HUGHES ENTERTAINMENT PRESENTS

GETTING IT

Dennis Hughes

ISBN: 978-1-951838-16-4

Acknowledgements

First, I want to thank the Almighty God for blessing me with this writing ability. I want to thank my kids for motivating me to get my ass up every day and do better. I would like to thank my team, Hughes Entertainment, for the support and helping me along the way. I want to thank Alona Hughes for saying, "man, gone and do it then." I just want to thank everybody who supported me through this process. Now, let's get to the book. I hope you enjoy reading it just as much as I had enjoyed the pleasure of writing it.

Table of Contents

Chapter 1

Lil Mike

"Hurry the fuck up, man, mama said get your ass down here now," I yelled a lie to my little brother because you know moms don't curse and all that.

She yelled over me, "Boy, I didn't say no such thing."

I said, "I wish your brother would hurry up."

Yeah, I just wanted to curse to see if I could get away with it. It was the day of the Lord, and mama always said, "The best way to get into heaven was to go to the house of the Lord," but I was sixteen and wanted to get out and do my own thing. I was the man of the house. Yeah, my pops went away, not to prison: just went away. You know the American dad story—my pops left to get some milk and never came back. Naw, fuck that shit! Big Mike, as they called him, was not going to get some milk. He was going to get some more pussy. That nigga had more kids than Jon and Kate plus eight, my dude.

I was the oldest of 14 and counting, so that's why I'm Lil Mike, aka Michael Montrell Beasley. I got my height from my dad: he was 6'6 and weighed over 300 pounds. He was quite the football player and all-around player in high school to college, from what I hear. He also had hoes galore. I remember riding with him one day over to Ms. Yasmin's house, and, man, he must have thought I was still a little boy because I heard her moaning like it was just too good to be true. But anyway, this dude was my hero for a

1

while, then he just up and told Mom he wasn't coming back, and he never did. Therefore, from that day forward, I was and still am the man of this house.

Growing up on Martin Luther King Drive was hard as fuck. We always had drama around the way. Why is it that any MLK anywhere in the world is bad? I mean, he was a good dude, so why is that? So, our church was filled with people acting like they had the holy ghost and all of that. I never understood that either, so you just stand up in front of the whole church and say God has gotten inside you. I mean, really? Every Sunday? Come on, man. I looked at my little brother, Joshua, and we just burst out and start laughing. And, of course, my mom just pinches us for laughing. So, we sit through another day of going to church, but I needed to tell mama that I couldn't go anymore because I really don't believe in Him. I mean, why are there killings everywhere you go and babies dying of diseases that man can't explain? So, I decided to be a man and told her I couldn't go anymore. So, after church, my little brother and I got dropped off at my cousin Tron's house. Now, this is my nigga until I die, you feel me? Tron and I fucked a few hoes at the same damn time, you feel me? We got drunk, robbed niggas, and the list goes on. My little brother Joshua tries to hang, but we use him as the lookout on every caper we pull. So, on this particular night, it was just the three of us, and we were bored, so you know what kids do on a night that they're bored. You've guessed right: we called some hoes and invited them over. My cousin was the opposite of me because I was 6" 1 and light skin like my pops. And this nigga was black as tar, had a belly at 17, and had a head full of waves with light eyes. He was my cousin, and I've never hated on anyone, but this nigga pulled hoes like nothing. We would walk into the mall and all these broads would go crazy. I never hated because Snoop said it best: "It's not fun if your niggas can have none." So, we tossed hoes to the side like tissue after we got done. So, after we called these broads, Brandy and Shauna, they came over and we all got high and drunk. Brandy was my main chick. I mean, man, she was bad as hell. She was high yella with titties and had an ass like a woman twice her age. And Shauna, her cousin, was just as fine, but not that cute in the face; however, that nigga Tron was feeling her hard. Brandy and I went into the room after sharing a few laughs with my cousin and my brother. You know me, I wanted the pussy. She was one of the females who thought sucking dick was nasty, but shit, I told her I needed it and put on the puppy dog look, and she fell for it every time. She was from the other side of the tracks. While I saw girls my age having two and three kids, crackheads were everywhere as drug dealers with fancy cars rode and you know the rest. She didn't grow up like us. She grew up in Hinesville and, man, did her pops have bread! I mean, long bread. He was this big shot attorney charging people $250 an hour just to work their cases. Yeah, he never lost a case, so I guess you get what you pay for. I remember her telling me she heard a few of her dad's conversations while talking to some of the people he knew was guilty. One day, she heard the guy tell her dad that if he doesn't win his case, everyone in his family will be dead in a matter of a week. Like I said, he never lost his case. But if he knew what his baby girl was about to do to me, man, he would have me tried for everything in the book and have me locked away for at least twenty to life. So, she was still talking 'bout she doesn't want to give me head, but I'm like, "Come on ma! Just do it this time." So, she finally gave in and did her thing. Just as I was about to let loose, we both hear a loud bang. I wanted to say, "Fuck it, keep going," but I knew I had to go see what the fuck was going on. So, I'm mad as shit right now: I put my pants on and we both went outside to see what the fuck is going on. And what we saw was like some old wild, wild west shit. Niggas was holding my cousins and brother by the fucking throat, asking where the money was. I pulled out my 38 and asked what the fuck was up in here, and, out of nowhere, a nigga hit me hard as fuck with a shotgun to the back of my head and I instantly fell to my knees. I got up and started to swing, but sometimes you got to pick your battles. So, I asked Tron what the fuck these niggas want and who are they.

This big black ass nigga who they were calling Ant said, "Nigga, we hear for the fucking money." Now, I did not understand what this nigga was talking about and I knew that nigga Tron didn't because we did everything together. Until I heard Tron say, "It's outside under the doghouse," I asked Tron what the fuck was going on. That nigga Ant said that nigga stole his money, and, after he got it, everybody who knew about it was going to die. And that nigga meant what he said—his henchmen came back in with two big ass black bags of money. Then, Ant looked at my little brother and asked if he knew anything. He shook his head and said, "No man, I swear I didn't know," so this nigga punched Josh in the mouth, and I was fucking furious, but these two niggas were holding me back. Finally, the nigga asked me if I knew.

I said, "Fuck you nigga." Next thing I knew, I heard the shot, and everything went black.

Chapter 2

Joshua

As we sat there waiting for my brother Lil Mike to come to this five-year reunion party for our cousin, Tron, I just sat and thought about that day. If Tron would've never taken that money from Ant, he would still be alive today. And Lil Mike would not have gotten shot that day. Something in him changed, and he was never the same. He is ruthless and doesn't give a fuck about anyone besides mama and me. He is now one of the most ruthless niggas you would come across. He does shit like leaving his car running while he's at the barbershop and dares someone to touch his shit. But towards his family, he could be the nicest nigga you would ever meet. So, while waiting on Lil Mike, my shorty Trice kissed me and asked me what was on my mind. I told her I was thinking about a few things. She said that a penny for your thoughts while flashing that sexy ass smile she has. She gets me every time with them dimples and them sexy Meagan Good lips. So, while I kissed her back, I looked around and thought to myself that I was glad that so many people came to the gathering for my cousin and his memory. This time each year always gets to a nigga because we can't live on ifs and whens. We just got to move on and try to cope as best as we can. I looked around and seen a few of the homies we grew up with and knew Tron on a personal level. I told Trice that I would be right back and asked if she wanted a drink. Of course, me and Lil Mike paid for this event. Tron's pictures hung around the event from when we were all together doing what we did best. So, I went around and dapped all the people that came out to this event and we just shot the shit and drank until I seen my brother walking in with this badass brown skin shorty. I mean, man, if he was sharing, I was getting with her and that's my word. I just had to see who this chick was and what she was about. I went over and dapped him up and asked who the lovely lady was. He said, "Damn nigga, stop slobbering over my shorty." They both start laughing. She reaches her hand and said her name was Alicia and it was nice to finally meet some of Lil Mike's people. He's been keeping her away, so I decided to fall back. We would usually finish and toss, but we've grown up from that since we were kids. We all sat down and had a good time, catching up on memories and talking shit until mama walks up and you know all the cursing stops immediately. She was still radiant, and we always had respect for her and how she raised up with no help. She was the poster child for an independent woman, and they say you want a woman like your mama. But she walks up and asks if we are having a good time and we all say yes and then introduce our dates to mama. She said, "Boys, you have good taste," and Trice and Alicia started blushing. They got up to hug mama like they were old friends. And it was important that mama liked who I was with for many reasons. I loved that lady like no one else in the world. After mama leaves, I asked Lil Mike to come holla at me about some business. We tell them we will be back and for them to order us some drinks.

Me and Lil Mike went outside on the terrace and I told him, "Man, you won't believe this shit." He didn't say anything, he just looked at me sideways because he knew I was in charge of this latest caper. We robbed drug dealers and didn't give a fuck. So, I told him what went wrong with the operation. He told me to start from the beginning. So, I told him it was Brian, Chris, and Tank all together and we all staked out this nigga named Head for about two weeks before we went in on that nigga. So, all four of us sat outside his crack house and looked at his day-to-day operations and that nigga Head was so fucking sloppy with his workers. They didn't have no skills, so I knew this shit would be easy. They kept the dope and the money in the same spots and them niggas wasn't really about gunplay. So, we just sat and waited: them lil niggas had hoes going in and out getting drunk and just sloppy as shit. The crack heads were standing around, making the spot hot as shit. So, we knew it would be an in and out. But shit, it didn't go as we planned. We looked at the spot long enough. So, Friday at 3 AM, we hit the spot when most of the hood was asleep. So, I took point and made sure everyone had their heat and masked with extra clips. Brian stayed in the car just in case we needed to make a quick getaway. He had the shotgun with him just in case we weren't back in thirty minutes flat. His order was to come in blasting no matter what. So, I went around the back and Tank kicked in the front door and, to our surprise, we only saw two bitches laying on the floor playing Uno cards. And we all looked around and no one said anything: they screamed and Tank told her to shut the fuck up before he blasts her to hell.

They asked the two females where the money was. They looked at each other and said nothing. Tank said, "I'm going to ask you bitches one more time where's the money." The light skin girl said it was in the room under the mattress. I pointed to Chris and told him to hurry up and go bag the shit up. I'm thinking to myself: *This is the easiest caper that we will ever do. No nigga's blood on our hands this time.* Just as we were about to leave, three niggas walked in and everything hit the fan. The short, dark skin nigga said to the hoes why they were laughing like it was funny. He looked at me and instantly drew his gun from his hip. Thank God I was a little quicker. I hit him twice in the chest before he knew what hit him. The other two niggas started dumping, so I jumped behind the couch to avoid getting shot. Just as I was about to start dumping, Tank came out the back with his twin Glocks hitting one of the other niggas in the shoulder, and he fell but didn't drop his weapon. He fired back and hit my nigga Tank in the head with a clean shot to the head. I see his fucking body fall; I instantly lose it, and I got up not giving a fuck about my life. I started shooting at the last nigga and hit him with two bullets to the head. His head splashes like a fucking grapefruit. I ran over to Tank and knew he was dead, and I had to leave his body because we were already over our time. I looked at Chris and he did not say anything: he just picked up the bags of money from the floor and said, "Rest in peace, nigga." He rushed outside and I had to do the only last thing that needed to be known. I shot both the girls point blank range on the bed. Shit, you know how it is: no witnesses, no murder trial. I ran downstairs to jump in the car. Brian looked at me and said, "He didn't make it, huh?" I looked at him and said, "Naw, my nigga: he didn't make it. Drive this motherfucker and let's be out." Little did we know that the nigga Head had cameras all hidden in the dope house because he didn't trust them niggas. So, he had all that shit that just transpired on camera and we were fucked. I took off my mask, so it was in his fucking hands.

I looked at Lil Mike and he looked at me with that big brother look like: N*igga, I told you so*. He just blew up on me and yanked me by my fucking collar. I told him, "Nigga, get the fuck off me." I knew this nigga was way stronger than me, so I just did the best I could to get this nigga off me. He let me go and stared in my eyes and told me, "Nigga, meet me at the spot in the morning and we will figure this bullshit out." We went back to the table, and I was sweating like a motherfucker because I never enjoyed letting my big brother down. But that nigga had to realize I was a grown ass man now. But I always wanted his respect.

Chapter 3

Lil Mike

Yes, I was mad as fuck at my brother for fucking up that caper. I let him run his first one and one of our most trusted soldiers got killed: fuck, I was heated. But as I laid beside my sexy lil mama, Alicia, I felt better. We went home that night and the way I had my shit set up impressed her. I never let females come to the crib, but it was something about her. She calmed the beast down inside me. She looked around my crib and said that my mama must've helped me. I laughed because she was right. I had a three-bedroom, three-bath crib on the outskirts of town that only three people (well, now, four people) knew about. As she looked around, she noticed a picture of Tron, my lil brother, and I sitting at the lake smiling and happy. She wanted to know a little more about me. Now, you know how a nigga is about all this feeling type of shit and opening up, but I told her to have a seat and asked if she liked anything to drink. She said that she would like to have just a coke, so I got it for her and made me a Hennessy straight on the rocks and we sat on the couch just chilling. I turned on the 80-inch flat screen on the wall, but neither one of us was watching it. She said she wanted to talk, but her eyes said another thing. She stood up and took off her shoes, and I knew it was about to go down. Yeah, she made a nigga wait and I'm glad she did because I would've probably lost interest if she gave it to me fast. So, she takes off her shirt and that sexy black bra she had on and instantly gets my dick hard. But, I play it cool and act like she just another chick, but, on the inside, I was like, *Fuck, she's so sexy to me.* She tells me to come here with her finger and I happily do what I am asked. I get up and go over to her and she kissed me like it was no tomorrow. She tiptoed to kiss me because I was way taller than her. Yeah, I got my height from Big Mike. I turned out to be 6'5 and weighing in over 250 pounds so I was a big dude. She sits me down on the couch and she takes off my shirt. She loved my tats: I had over 25 tats from my neck to my legs. She kisses my chest and grabs my dick. She looks at me like she approved of my dick. I just smiled because she made me wait, so I knew I had to fuck Alicia right when she gave me a chance. So, she sits between my legs and unzips my pants. She takes my dick out and she gasps. This was nothing new because I had twelve inches strong and not a lot of females could take all this dick. So, she proceeds to lick the head slowly, just like I like, while looking me in my eyes. They were telling me: *Nigga, I'm going to take this dick.* She proceeds, licking my dick all slow and sensual like she had a nice lollipop that she's been waiting to suck it. She licks from the base of my dick and makes slurping noises that drives me wild. She then takes as much as she could in her mouth without choking, to my surprise: she sucks in at least eight inches and it drove me wild. She then played with my balls, jiggling them like only she could. She then stops all a sudden and asked if I had condoms. I looked at her stupid and said they were in my top drawer in my bedroom.

I grabbed her hand and she followed me to my master bedroom which was set up with a California king size bed with a flat screen and surround sound that I hooked up myself. I also had mirrors on the ceiling because I loved to watch when these females were riding me and trying to take this dick I had to offer. I laid her down on the bed, and I wanted to taste that pussy as soon as I saw it. She took off her pants and I was in awe. She was neatly shaved and had the prettiest pussy that I have ever seen. I played with her pearl tongue like it was no tomorrow. I licked her slowly at first, then sped up when she started bucking and she was calling the man's name in vain. I just started thinking to myself: *Damn, her pussy tastes so good.* So, I turned her over for her to get on all fours and ate her from the back: she lost her mind. She was fucking my tongue like it was no tomorrow. She came hard and I licked it all up. She was exhausted from that nut, but I was just getting started. I walked over to the drawer and put the XL magnum on and go back to her and she already has her legs up waiting for this dick. I entered her slowly and her pussy was so tight just like the way I liked it. A wet, tight pussy was the way to a nigga's heart. Don't get me wrong, food is good too, but a good, clean pussy is the shit. I eased inside her with slow strokes, and she tried to throw the pussy back, but I eased as much dick inside her as she could take: she told me not to stop no matter how she screamed for me to stop. Her nails were digging into my back and I knew it was pain in my back, but all I could think about is digging inside this pussy. She told me she was about to cum for the third time and I just got deeper and deeper until she said she can't

13

take anymore from that position so I flipped her over and eased this dick in her box and she threw it back like a horse. Her ass was so fucking sexy: no scars—just a sexy ass body. I couldn't take anymore, so I busted all up inside her and she was cumming again as I was. We both leaned over, not saying anything. So, I broke the silence and asked if she wanted to take a shower with me. We both get up and headed to the bathroom to shower. We got out the shower and headed to the living room. I got a call on my cell phone, so I went to the bedroom to answered it. It was business and none of Alicia's business, so I did her a favor. I answered the phone and, to my surprise, it was that nigga Head saying he wanted a meeting with me and my brother tomorrow at noon. He said to bring two hundred and fifty stacks for the tapes or they might find their way to the police.

I said to that bitch ass nigga, "So you going to tell on my fucking brother?"

He replied, "Nigga, you all started this shit; I'm just going to finish it," and he hung up.

I said: "Fuck," and called Josh to let that him know to get up the bread to give to this bitch ass nigga. Josh told me to fuck that nigga and he's not giving his hoe ass anything.

I calmly stated: "Nigga, you fucked this one up, so you got to go in that stash and give that bitch what he wants."

"We got to get the drop on him."

I said, "Josh, shut the fuck up and get the money ready because I have a plan," then I hung up. All I wanted to do was get some pussy, but now I couldn't enjoy it be-cause that nigga was always doing crazy shit.

Chapter 4

Alicia

I gave this nigga some head and some of this pussy, and he was up in there talking on the phone probably to another bitch. I can't even get mad because it's my fault that I feel like this. When I first met Lil Mike at the mall, I wasn't even looking for a mark that day. It just happened and I'm not even mad: I guess fate is real. I was in there with my girl Reva and we were just sitting at the food court—not even looking that nigga's way until he caught my eye. It's hard to miss this tall, handsome man. I was like: *Damn, I might have to get my rent paid by this nigga.* So, I was on that day: shit, I'm on every day. But that day, I was dressed casually in my red polo shirt and with my True Religion jeans and the red and white J's on my feet. That bitch Miley Cyrus doesn't have shit on me in the J's department. Now, most of mine was stolen, but she still couldn't fuck with me. So, I saw him looking at some shoes in FootLocker, so I told Reva to come on and let's go. She hollers about I'm not done yet. I said, "Bitch, after I'm done with this nigga, I'll get you a restaurant." We both laughed because somehow, we knew that nigga had money and knew what money looked like. So, we casually walked in acting like we didn't even see that nigga. So, he came over to me and said, "Ma, you need some help?" I looked at him and said, "Yes, can I see those in a size 6.5, please?" He looked at me like I'm a joke because his boys laughed at him. They were saying, "Damn Lil Mike, she played you." Reva cracked a smile also, and he flashed a smile and told me he could buy me the store if I wanted it. I politely told him no thanks and walked out of the store. I knew this was a sure-fire plan he would come after me. And, as sure as my name is Alicia, he said, "Excuse me, miss: can I talk to you for a second." I looked at my watch and told him he had one minute to impress me. He smiled at me and I almost melted, but he would never know that. So, he was going on about how he would like to take me out and wine and dine me. So, I gave in and let him have the pleasure of knowing a real go getter bitch like me. Any man would be lucky to have me on their team and that's why I treated my time as such. So yeah, I gave him the number and said to call me when he was not around all his goons. So, he called three days later: now, what I do is set these niggas up and give them a run for their money. Literally, I give them a run for their money because when I set these niggas up, they be running their pockets until they are bone dry. I might have to give up the pussy sometimes, but it's all worth it. I set them up and my cousin Head gets their money. Now he is a dope boy and just doing his thing so far, but we together pull in good numbers. He just got hit up a few weeks ago and no one knows who did it, but I guess the streets like that. Lil Mike has become my boo. I haven't asked him for anything. I let him know that I have my own and don't need him for shit. When I pulled that nigga pants down, I almost shitted a brick because he had the biggest dick I have ever seen. And, man, was it good, but that nigga would never know that. So, I decided not to set this nigga up this time, but, if he gets out of line, then he will be broke just like the rest of these niggas. So, whoever he was on the phone in that room doesn't have anything on me and I intend to keep it like that.

Chapter 5

Josh

I'd tried to tell my damn brother, "Man, fuck Head! I'm not giving this nigga shit. He wants to be a snitch ass nigga: that isn't my fault." He is talking bout he has a plan, but I wondered what the fuck he came up with. He must realize I am not his little brother anymore. Yeah, he will always be my older brother, but we are not kids anymore. So, early the next morning, I heard pounding at my apartment and I was mad as fuck because I was up all night thinking how I could kill this nigga Head for even thinking this was a police involvement. But there is no honor amongst thieves, so fuck it. I guess I had to listen to what Lil Mike had to say. I opened the door and there's my brother asking me if I got the money yet. I looked at him and said, "No, big bro, I think we should...," but, before I got another word out, he said, "I didn't ask you to think, Josh: we got to get that nigga that money man. We will get that shit back one way or another, but right now, I have a plan that is set into motion about this nigga Head." Just get the bread and meet at the spot at 2:30 PM: he just fucking walked out without saying another word. Fuck man, I lost my nigga over this bullshit, so I owe it at least to him to kill this nigga Head as soon as I see that nigga. But, I guess I got to at least meet Lil Mike at the spot. It was only 9:30 AM, so I had to shower and change and still had time to get the money up for this bitch.

As I hopped in my money green Impala, one 24's with 4 twelve's and 6 screens I burned off. You know it's me when I do because I beat down the block every time I come through any hood. So, I turned up my Kevin Gates, lit a blunt, and went to get that money that we had taken from so many other niggas that wasn't really deserving of that money anyway. So, did I feel bad for robbing this dude out here that is shining the wrong way? Shit, if I had respect for someone, my rule was that I wouldn't rob my nigga. But these niggas are about themselves: they don't do shit for anyone but themselves and that shit isn't right. As I rolled up to the spot where I hid most of my money, I rode past it four times just to make sure I wasn't being followed. I got my burner out of my hidden contraction under the seat and went inside to get the money. It was a little apartment I had in this ducked off neighborhood. Nobody knew about this place but two people alive: my brother and I. I got the money and hit Lil Mike up and told him that I would be there in 20.

Chapter 6

Lil Mike

As we all made it to the spot, we looked at each other and said nothing to one another. We went somewhere that is hiding in plain sight, which is in the back of Sue's Cleaners. It was the perfect place to hide money, and we all had uniforms as if we worked there. It was owned by this old man named Harrold; he was this older Black cat who was a no-nonsense cat about stupid shit. As long as we broke him off to keep this place going, he was happy and didn't give a fuck what we did or to who. He named the business after his old lady who passed like ten years back, and he always wanted to keep it open to honor her. So, I respected him for that shit. The four of us looked at each other and wondered why I told them to be here when this is not our day to meet. We usually met every Thursday at 4 PM no matter what we had going on. And this would be the first one without Tank attending this meeting. I had a bottle of Patron on ice that I told Harold to have ready in the backroom before we got there. As usual, he came through for me again. I told them to take a shot glass and we all poured one out for Tank. Brian, Chris, Josh, and Lil Mike are all we had now to carry out the plans. So, we had to get it regardless of the situation or circumstance.

"So, Brian: you go by Tank's mama's house and tell her we got that funeral cost and whatever she needs to make it through this." After taking a few more shots and smoked good, I stood up and laid out my plan for this nigga Head and his henchmen. All ears were open, and it was so quiet, you could hear a mouse pissing on cotton. Just as I was about to say what I had planned for him, my cell phone rings from an unknown caller and I already knew who it was. I placed it on speakerphone so the crew could hear how this nigga was playing a reckless game and didn't even know it.

I say *yeah* into the phone.

He asked, "Nigga, do you have my money yet or should I call the laws right now and ask if they want to solve an unsolved case?" At this point, I'm fucking heated, but I don't show it in front of the crew because that would show weakness. I kept my composure and said, "Yeah, nigga: we got your money." He said, "This is where I want you pussies to put my money at: in front of the tire shop on South Ninth by the dollar store. I'm pretty sure you broke ass niggas know where that is," and he proceeded to laugh. I didn't see a fucking thing funny, but I had to play my position well about this hoe ass nigga. I said that is a fuck load of money to be walking around with in a trash bag. He said, "Put it in the trash can in front of the building." I asked where the tapes were. This was an exchange, so he needed to be giving me those tapes. He screamed into the phone that he was in charge and I don't make demands. "Just do as I fucking say, and you bitches won't get to jail behind killing my niggas. So, bitches drop the money off at no later than 10 PM tonight. If you're even a few seconds late, the deal is off. And trust me, nigga, if anything happens to me or my goons, I made a copy to send to the police; therefore, if we have any problems and I don't make it back, they know what to do with the tapes," and he hung up. By this point, Josh's veins are popping out his neck and so is Brian's and Chris'. They all looked at me like what's the plan now? I told them that the plans have changed.

Chapter 7

Head

Yeah, I had them bitch ass niggas exactly where I wanted them, and I was about to recover my fucking money that I took an L on. But I could care less about the money, and I could've taken the L, but it was the principle of the shit and how it was done. I know the game and leaving no witnesses is the rules of this game. But for them niggas to kill my damn niece and her friend that was crossing the lines. My brother was killed in jail and I made a promise to him and I couldn't keep it. I let his daughter around danger, and she got killed over some bullshit. She was barely sixteen and I am hurting to this day about the shit. I am torn up inside about my niece. So, I got to kill two of theirs because, if you kill one of mine, I got to come back two times harder. So, yeah: fuck them niggas and they bitch ass don't even realize that it was never any tapes in that trap house. I had been planning on getting a camera system in that spot, but an old school told me not to because if the police were to ever kick in my shit while I was watching the tapes, that isn't nothing but evidence against yourself and the ones you are trying to protect. So, I told them niggas to drop the money off to my uncle's tire shop because I knew my uncle would get the money and put the money away for me until I needed it. And when he got the money, I would have him hold up three blank tapes in the air and drop them in the trash can and burn them as to say:

This is the last of the tapes. Those niggas would fall for that shit. Especially that nigga Josh: I never liked that nigga, anyway. I mean, these niggas out here robbing niggas. I understood the shit, but I just didn't want to be the one to be on the other end of that shit. But I guess what goes around, always comes back. I was on my own after my brother went to jail for me. I got pulled over with two guns in the car and he took the charge for me and made me promise that I would take care of my niece and I couldn't even keep that promise. And, after he got killed in jail, I almost lost my fucking mind. My cousin Alicia is the only reason that I made it on the real. She was like me and my brother, she grew up without shit. So, when she got older and she filled out, I thought of this setting up niggas idea and she was the perfect person to do that. She was very pretty and had a body that most niggas fell for and that's why the shit was so fucking easy to these lame ass niggas. They put pussy on a pedestal and that's where they end up: falling over the shit. I mean, good pussy is always good, but knowing you can take care of your family and giving them what they need and want is better than any pussy in the world. Fuck, how was I going to tell her that my niece is dead? Guess it's time for us to have another meeting.

Chapter 8

Alicia

Reva and I were downtown shopping in the mall when I got a call from Head. I knew it was money time, so I answered in a hurry. "What it do, big cuz? What you up to?" He had this sound in his voice to let me know that this wasn't a money call. He started with: "Hey shorty, we need to talk ASAP. When can you meet me at the crib?" So, I was panicking because he never sounded like that, so I asked him, "What's wrong, Head: tell me what's up." He said: "Naw, I got to go handle some business so meet me at the crib in an hour," and he hung up. So, I looked at Reva and told her I must take her home and she was mad because she didn't get to get those red bottoms that she wanted. I said that I would bring her back when I finished with my cousin. So, we left the mall, and I dropped off Reva and told her I would hit her up later. She said that I better and gave me a smile that drove most niggas crazy and I just laughed. So, I would stop by the house, but I wanted to see what Head had to say. So, as I pulled up to the house, my cell phone rang and it was Lil Mike. I smiled because that nigga had me open, but I would never let him know that. I answered and asked what he was up to. He said he thought about me and decided to hit me up. I smiled from ear to ear and said let me find out you really like me. I could sense that he is smiling on the other end. He asked when he could see me again and that he wanted to chill that night depending on what I was doing. I told him nothing but that I didn't want to make it seem like I was sitting around waiting on him even though I was. Again, he would never know that. So, I told him I would meet him at his house at around 9 PM. We said our goodbyes and then we hung up.

I sat in the car for a few minutes and thought about could I really settle down and have roots somewhere and could I be truly happy? I walked up to my cousin's apartment and I took a deep breath to get ready for whatever conversation we had to have. I knocked on the door and the bolts come undone. And I asked myself why this dude still stay here in the projects because he was fucking breaded up. When I say this nigga had to be worth well over 15 million. But every time I asked, he always said, "I'mma die in the hood," which was stupid but it is what it is. I walked in and could tell he had been drinking because it was two glasses like he expected to tell me something bad. So, he asked me if I would like a drink and I passed on the drink. I asked what was up and he came out with it. He told me that Arianna is dead. I looked at him like he's crazy. A tear comes down my cheek and then he looks at me with sorrowful eyes and then the tears pour down my cheeks and I asked him what happened to her and he told me the story but he left out the names of the people who actually did it. I guess he was trying to protect me from what was going on in this big fucked- up world. He just told me that he got a clue that this nigga named Josh did it. Man, it was 500 hundred niggas named Josh in the world. So, I just looked at him and asked what about his brother and that he made a promise to him that he would keep her safe

27

and he let her die by having her in a fucking trap house. He looked at me and started to fucking yell at the top of his lungs: "You don't think I fucking know that shit, Alicia. I'm hurting and I know that I fucked up with my niece's life! I haven't slept since the shit happened." He started to say something else and his voice trailed off into a whisper. I went over to him and hugged big cuz for a minute and told him that everything would be alright. And I left him there and told him that I would check on him later. I went to my car and cried harder because she never had a chance. Her mama was killed at a red light by a drunk driver and her daddy was in jail for going and killing the woman that killed her in the drunk driving accident. He went to jail and not too long after, he got killed in jail and now she was dead. She was just at odds with her life, but it's just the way the cookie fucking crumbled, I guess. I needed to get my head right, so I headed to my house and lit a blunt to get my head right.

Chapter 9

Lil Mike

I told them niggas to be ready at nine that night and that we would meet up at the spot to all drive in separate cars. I had a plan, but this nigga was talking about crazy shit, so I had to come up with another plan to beat this nigga at his own game. I was on my way to go meet my nigga about an issue I had him investigate. He was a real computer geek, so I always kept him around. The thing about me I like to know every bitch I fuck with. So, I had him investigate Alicia Taylor, and he said he came up with a few things about her. I wasn't surprised because I didn't trust any bitch on any level. So, he said she spent a few months on a possession charge and had probation for stealing out of Wal-Mart, which is crazy because she acts like she just comes from money. I mean, I really started feeling this chick, so I had to check her out. He also told me I wanted to see this: she had an abortion at thirteen and I was shocked like a motherfucker to find that shit out. I didn't judge anyone, but this was on a different level. I mean, where I'm from, females were having babies in junior high and by the time they were seniors, they were taking their babies to school. But I would have to ask her about her past and I know people don't have to share, but I'm different. I want to know everything about you and no surprises. She told me she only had a few people down here and other than that, she was by herself. So, I made a note to holler at her about it. She didn't know I was shot, so I guess we would have to get all that shit right. Even though I was 21, I had been through a lot of fucked-up shit. So, I told him I appreciated it and I would hit him up later. It was almost time to head to the spot, so I hopped in my blue F-150 Texas Edition pickup truck on 28's. My shit was stupid, and I was the only youngster riding around in this color. So, I knew if a nigga would try to steal my shit or even want to try some shit, they would get the business and that's my word. I finally pulled up to the spot, but something was wrong: I had this bad feeling that came over me. I called Josh to see where he was at and got no answer. So, I called Brian and Chris and got no answer either. So, by this time, I'm heated. I waited for a little while after nine and start riding around.

Chapter 10

Josh

Yeah, I hit Brian and Chris on the hip and told them to meet me at my spot because I had something to holler at them about. And Chris asked if we were supposed to meet my brother at the spot in a few. I told him we should, but I had another plan I think would work and would be over with all this bullshit. So they came, and I said to them that we could sit there and be played, or we could go get this nigga by surprise and go to his crib and kill that nigga before he even knows what happens to him. We could go in his crib and kill this nigga, man, and take all the rest of his shit. And as always, my niggas were down with the shit. So, I figured we would be in and out and this problem would be taken care of in a matter of fifteen minutes tops and no one would be killed. So, we all piled in Chris' old school 'Lac and rode to this nigga's apartment, but when we got there with the burners out and about to go in, I saw a very familiar face I instantly recognized, and I told them to hold up. It was my brother's bitch, Alicia, coming out of the apartment and I said to myself: *What the fuck could she be doing coming out of this apartment and crying like that.* So, I told them the plan is off and we headed back to the car. They looked at me confused and asked what the fuck my problem was: "I thought we was going in to get this nigga and get it over with." So, I told them that the bitch that just came out of Head's apartment is Lil Mike's bitch.

They looked at each other and just asked what the fuck was going on. "I think that nigga Head is trying to set up my brother with that bitch. I don't know how and when, but check it out: neither one of you'll say anything to Lil Mike about this shit. I want to check this shit out and see what this bitch is about. So, for now, let's meet Lil Mike and go along with his plan for now. Agreed?" They both shook their heads, and we all rode in silence to meet Lil Mike.

Chapter 11

Lil Mike

So, I finally caught up with these niggas and asked where the fuck had they been and what took so fucking long. Of course, my brother answered first and said they had to take care of something. I just said fuck it and left it alone, but I just wanted to get the shit over with. We all hopped in two cars to give this nigga the money that he demanded for my brother's fuck up. So, we made it there and I parked across the street and everyone is mostly gone from the area except for a few patrons leaving work for the night. I looked at my watch and it was 9:50 PM so I told Chris to get the bag and put it in the trashcan and make sure no one was looking. So, he walked across the street and put it in the trash can as instructed. He ran back across the street and, as if on cue, Head's uncle comes out of the tire shop and gets the black bag out of it. He raised up two black tapes, put them in the trash, put lighter fluid in it and proceeded to burn them as Head said. He lifted the bag as if to say: *Nice doing business with you bitches*. I waited for the call to come through from Head's bitch ass. About 10:15 PM, I got the call from him and he said, "It looks like it's all there so you pussies can leave and go about your business but just wanted to let you know that this shit is not over with pussies," and then he hung up. What that bitch ass nigga didn't know that I knew he was there at the tire shop the whole time and he was inside. It was just a matter of time that this nigga fell into my trap that I had set up for his bitch ass. Now, I have never been a snitch or a hoe ass nigga: I had to get rid of him somehow, but I wanted to embarrassed this nigga even though it's my brother who had started this shit. But I was with my brother right or wrong: that's how we rolled. Once that nigga came out running in the street with a blue face, we drove off laughing. What he didn't know was that I had a bitch at the bank that I fucked on a regular and I had to fuck her real good to get some of that blue spray that sprays in your face after you rob a bank and don't come off with only this solution that only hospitals have. So, it looked like he robbed a bank. The only way he could get that shit off is to go to the hospital and get that medical solution. I told that nigga not to fuck with me on some crazy shit. So as we drove off laughing at that nigga with a blue face, I stayed thinking of how that nigga didn't have the money or his dignity and I figured that this shit is going to mean war and we had to be ready for whatever and whenever it came in. So, I told that nigga to drop me off at my car and I'd hit them up later.

Chapter 12

Alicia

It was 3 AM, and this nigga had the nerve to call me back when he was the one who asked me to chill. Before I went to sleep, I was heated like a motherfucker. Now I'm not stupid by far: I knew he had other hoes but, when we were together, he treated me like someone and I liked that about him. I really liked this dude, but, as of tonight, he was fucking up. I just needed to be held because my lil cousin was dead and just wanted to be in his strong arms. I had a hard exterior, but I was soft as cotton on the inside, but you would never know. So, I answered the phone with an attitude until I heard this nigga's sexy baritone voice: inside, I just melt, but I'm acting like I'm mad, but I'm smiling on the inside. So, I went off on this nigga and asked why the hell he wanted to talk now: he was the one who asked me to chill, and if he had other engagements, all he had to do was let me know. He cut me off and said to open the door and I'm like, "What the fuck?" because I never told this nigga where I stayed and I say, "Yeah right, I never told you where I live so how are you even at my door?" I looked out my peep hole and dropped the phone because I am looking crazy with my hair all over my head. I have no mouthwash and no make-up even though I didn't need it, but the fact he just popped up at my crib when I never told him where I stayed. So, I told him to hold on for a second as I rushed to the bathroom to put on my robe and brush my hair in a ponytail and put some mouthwash in my mouth and swish it around just to make sure my breath is sweet just in case that nigga trying to get some ass. So, I rushed back to the door and answered it. This nigga had the audacity to just walk in and kiss me. I could taste Hennessy on his breath mixed with maybe spearmint gum and this nigga sent chills up my spine, and instantly, my panties got soaked, he closed the door and still didn't say a word. It was like I was trapped in a great dream and couldn't get up. Not that I wanted to, but I didn't want to give this nigga all the power, but the way he touched me had me on another level. He pushed me back into the apartment and slid his hands all over my body: I felt like I was in heaven. He picked me up and we kissed stronger than we ever had. I could tell it was the liquor mixed with my sexy body that this nigga needed to bust this nut. While he had me in the air, we were bumping into the wall while knocking a few over but at that point, I didn't even care the way he handled my body. We made it to the bedroom, and he plopped me on the bed while kissing on my neck that he knows is one of my spots and he slightly bites it, driving me fucking wild. He pulled my shirt over my head exposing my 38 C-cups out with dime size nipples exposed. He licked one gently while flicking the other one slightly just like I liked it. I don't know how this nigga knew my body like it's his own, but, at that moment, he could have anything he wanted, and he didn't even know. Shit, maybe he did. He came to my house and I never even told him he could or even where I stayed. Then, he ripped my green boy shorts off and sticks two fingers inside and feels how wet I am and he looks at me and smiles. To my surprise, this nigga picked me up in mid-air and proceeded to eat my pussy like it's his last meal—at first, I was worried about him dropping me, but, after five seconds or so, I realized he wouldn't let me fall. So, I relaxed, and he tears into my pussy like he was going to jail tomorrow, and that would be his last time. Now, I've done some freaky shit, but I have never had my kitty eaten while in the air and enjoying it. He made circle motions to my clit while every so often he dips his tongue in and out of my box. I told him *right there* and *don't stop* and he listened to my command like a good soldier that he was. After about two more minutes, I'm about to climax all over his face saying *oh God, I'm cumming; right there, baby, please don't stop, right there* and I finally release and I feel like in these few seconds I black out from the feeling on this nigga's tongue and I felt so good, I told him to put me down. I was so exhausted and I remember this nigga's dick was about to stretch me out again. He was by far the best lover I had ever had and, if I could, I would fuck him every day of the week. It was so good that I let all the other lames I had go and that's saying something because I don't trust any niggas and that's my word. So, I heard him unzip his pants and I knew what time it was. I told him to grab a Magnum from my dresser and, in one move, he moved to the dresser and got one. He picked it up and put it on: my pussy was so wet that he slipped in without any hesitation, but he didn't get all the way in. He had to work it in and out and I am in heaven again and before you know it, I am cumming again. I could feel him all up in my guts, but, like a big girl, I took all that shit and threw that pussy back to him and he tried not to moan, but that nigga was saying his *ohhs* and *ahhhs* and I knew he was in heaven also because I know this pussy is good. He pushed my legs all the way up to my ears and I felt him hitting spots I didn't know I had, but I had to take that shit. I pushed him over to ride that big dick and I went in, and I rode him backward. He loved the way I gripped my pussy muscles tight as I continue to ride him. I can tell he was about to bust, so I did the unthinkable and pulled his dick out and took his condom off and sucked him dry and swallowed every bit until he was dry as a bone while jiggling his balls at the same time. After he cums inside my mouth, I continued to suck on the head and he was still whimpering like a baby, so I continued until he tapped my head telling me to stop. I got up and went to the bathroom to wash my mouth out and get him a towel to wash his dick and balls even though there was nothing left to wash but I still did it. I walked out the room and the nigga was in the refrigerator drinking juice like that nigga from the movie *Baby Boy*. So I say, "You want to tell me why you are here at my house?" He said, "Because I am going to make you mine," and then he got dressed and left and I'm like what the fuck.

Chapter 13

Josh

Man, when I say that shit was funny what Lil Mike did to that nigga, I laughed my fucking ass off. I would've never thought to do that shit. When he came out running with a blue face looking like them blue men from that Las Vegas show, man, we drove off I was laughing at the nigga because I knew when he realized what we did, he was going to be mad than a bitch. Oh well, like I've always said: *There is no honor amongst thieves.* Head and his uncle came out of that shop trying to rush his bitch ass to the hospital from that shit the people be having when they robbed the bank. My damn brother came up with a genius ass idea to put that shit in that damn bag with the money. I just wish I was in the damn shop when he opened the damn bag. So, I know what we did was wrong, but trying to get us back by fucking with our bread was not the way to go. I decided to call it a night fucking with these goons. Time to go get some pussy.

Chapter 14

Head

Man, fuck these bitch-made niggas, man: they had me up in the hospital looking stupid like I robbed a fucking bank or something. It's all on my face and my uncle's face. For some reason, these bitch ass fuck boys decided to double-cross me. I said to myself and my uncle, *I told you them bitches would pay us.* As soon as we opened the bag, *BOOM.* Three fucking squirts of blue liquid come spouting out, and I was temporarily blinded. That shit got me and my uncle at that point. It stained all the fucking money. As I sat in the fucking hospital room, nobody wanted to help me because I know these fucking nurses knew the procedure of what happens when somebody comes in the hospital with blue liquid on their faces. As I sat in the waiting room, two cops came in and laughed and talked to each other. Just then, my uncle walked past him and asked me if I wanted anything to drink. They immediately drew their weapons right there in the fucking hospital and told us to lie on the ground. I'm getting more heated because all of this because a group of fuck boys robbed me and got in my business. They came and handcuffed us and I knew the procedure. Me and my uncle laid down and asked what we are being detained for and they told us that we have been implemented in a crime with that special dye pack on our face. I asked if we could just get help first because we tried to get that shit off and it would not come off. That's when he looked at his partner and said this dumbass doesn't know that the hospital is the only place that has the solution to get the dye off his face and then the police are notified. Again, at that point, I'm getting incredible hulk mad and I just wanted to smash something. They stood us both up and took pictures of us. Then, took us to the back to get the dye packs off our faces and take us to jail. As we were taken to the police car, I sat in that bitch and told my uncle on my dead niece that I won't sleep until all of them bitches are dead.

Chapter 15

Lil Mike

I know she's probably wondering how the fuck I knew where she stayed, and I don't really give a fuck. It's my job to know who I am dealing with, especially with my line of work. After my cousin Tron got killed, I really changed in different ways. Well, that's what everybody says though, I just figured this was inside me all along and it just came out. I was always that dude who spoke my mind on an issue if I didn't feel like what you were talking about wasn't real. For instance, I hate when a fuck boy is talking, and you know he's lying. That shit right there burns me and sometimes it's just hilarious how a mother fucker could just sit here and make up some shit like it's nothing wrong with that. I was still learning about Alicia so that getting to know me all the way was out of the question until I knew way more about her. She had dope clothes and an apartment and her own car, but hell, I've never seen her go to work a day since I met her and wondered where the fuck she got all that money. Now, I am a real dude, so I didn't question her until she stated that she got money out of these niggas to her friend raven. So, my fucking ears burned as I wanted to do more investigating on her. I didn't come up with anything, but I just always wanted to have a family like five boys running around and maybe one daughter. Hell, I wouldn't mind having twins then two singles. I didn't have my pops Big Mike like that

42

in my life so I promised myself I would always be in my kid's life. To be honest, I knew she acted like she didn't like the dick and the head I'd been giving her, but I read her body and you can't hide that shit. I went to her house and wanted her to know that it's deep when I'm fucking with you because I have trust issues. She knows that I have other females that I fuck with. That's not the genuine reason I went over here though: the actual reason I went over there was because I needed a place to lay my head that night and that was just the place that I chose for the night. Now you know when a nigga is stressed, head is the best remedy to all those problems, at least for the time being. I told her to come over and come chill with me; she said *Hold on and let me roll you this blunt quick for you.* At that point, I was smiling on the inside, but I wanted them lips bad. So, she comes over to me, passes the blunt, and I light it up. I take a few pulls and look at her looking at me all sexy in them blue boy-shorts and a t-shirt thicker than cold peanut butter. I passed her the blunt and we are chilling, and soon as she starts to unzip my pants, her phone goes off. She didn't answer the first time, but somebody was blowing her shit up. I said, "Fuck man, answer your fucking phone." She smacked her lips and went to get her phone and asked, "Who the fuck is this?" *You have a collect call from Head at the Ouachita Correctional Facility.* She dropped her phone and I'm like *What the fuck is going on now*?

Chapter 16

Alicia

I dropped the phone because I was high, and I wanted to know what the fuck was going on. If I knew my cousin and I do, I didn't understand why he was locked up. That was the most cautious and careful person I know. I heard Head say Alicia needed to wake the fuck up if she was asleep. I told him that I was here and up! He said that he needed me to go to 191 South Third and ask for Peanut because he needed to get up out that bitch. I asked him what the fuck happened. He said he was set up by some bitch made ass niggas and he would take care of the shit. I asked him when I got on South Third, what the fuck should I do, and he said ask Peanut. He told me to get the bond money from Peanut and bring it to the bail bondsman. He then asked if I got it and then told me that my uncle was also in jail. I'm like, "What the fuck did uncle do? What do you have him in?" *You have one minute left for the phone call,* the lady said on the phone. "Just go get that money from Peanut and get me out this bitch tomorrow; we need you," and then he hung up. After we got off the phone, Lil Mike looked at me sideways and thinking God knows what. He looked at me and asked what I got going on. I said that's just family drama as usual. I knew that nigga was about to start tripping so, I pushed him on the couch, and he gave me this puppy dog look like he knew he was about to get a treat. Hell, my head game is a treat within itself. So,

I pulled down his boxers and just stared at big monster. I still couldn't believe how big his dick was. I started to stroke it slowly and he was still looking at me like he wanted me to devour that damn thing. I started jacking it slowly looking him in his eyes, then I spat on it real slow. I let the spit run from my tongue to his head of his dick then I sucked the spit back up and did that three times and that nigga lost his mind. I knew I had him right where I wanted him. After teasing him a little, hell, I sucked his head slowly and squeezed his balls at the same time. Sucking the head while jacking his dick was a sure-fire way to make him bust quick; hell, my jaw was hurting from trying to stretch to his dick. He grabbed my head and tried to make me deep throat it so I let him fuck my face until it couldn't go any deeper. His head started to throb, so I knew he was about to bust; I squeezed his balls harder and looked him in the eyes while I swallowed every fucking drop. This man came so hard down my throat and I didn't complain one bit. I kept sucking after he busted because I knew what he liked; plus, he got back hard fast and I wanted some dick. I stood up and pulled off my boy-shorts that he loved to see my ass jiggle in. I bent over on the couch and kept my ass up but my face down just like he liked it. He didn't have a con-dom so I said fuck it. I guess I was getting the meat raw that night. I arched my back and waited for the dick and it was worth the wait. He just put the head in, and he loved it when I threw it back without him telling me. So, I fucked him like I was mad at him. He had that dick a bitch would fight over and cut a bitch if I had to, but he will never know that. I'm threw it back and took most of the dick like a champ and that dick was feeling good as he pulled out of me and flipped me over on my back like a ragdoll and put the head back in and beat this pussy up like he knew the world was coming to an end. After that last nut, I was fucking done and just wanted to go to sleep. I was so glad he was about to bust again. He wore me the fuck out and I just wanted to go to sleep. He pulled out and busted all over my titties and I didn't even care at that point because he fucked me into a damn slumber. He rolled over and we dozed off. I woke up to my phone going off and Lil Mike was gone.

Chapter 17

Josh

I woke up to banging at my door and I grabbed my gun because, every other day, I think I am going to get got. I know that's not how I am supposed to be living, but you know how that shit goes. So, I got my gun and went to the door. I looked thru the peephole and it's that nigga Brian and he got a look on his face to say he's scared. I opened the door and say, "Nigga, get your ass in here and why the fuck are you banging on my shit so loud?" He gave me a pound and he started to tell somebody to get to his mom at the grocery store and I'm like, "Wait, hold up; back up." He told me somebody rolled up to his mama getting out the car, pulled their dick out and pissed on his mama's shoes and I'm like, "Wait; what?" He told me to make a long story short, a nigga told his mama after taking his dick out and pissing on her to tell that bitch ass son of hers that this is only the beginning and pushed her down. "Now I have to kill the entire city if I must, brah." Man, when I say that shit was crazy as fuck to me and we were going to ride against whoever it was. You don't get at a nigga's mama, especially when I knew who the nigga was working for. That motherfucker Head was going to get got again because I knew where another one of his spots was. "Shit, we can do that tonight if you want to. Just let me hit Lil Mike and clear it with him." "Man, Josh, fuck that; this nigga done sent a nigga and pissed on my mama's shoes. Man, you know how fucking humiliating that shit is?"

"Okay, okay, brah; I feel you. Go and get the crew and meet me at the 76 store on Winnsboro Road." He dapped me up and left. *Fuck, man, that shit is crazy,* I thought to myself. I went back in the room and Trice was looking at me crazy. She knew when something was about to go down and I didn't want to hear that bitching about my business. I told her that I did not want to hear that shit and she said that she was not even saying anything. I asked if she had seen my phone, and she told me, "Nigga, no," with an attitude? I just hopped in the shower and mashed out. I got on my Kawasaki 1500 and headed to the west, where my brother and I had a crib that nobody knew about. It's a place on Finks' Hideaway Road where it's mostly white. I walked into the house and heard a noise coming from the back; I grabbed my gun out of my pants and walked in slowly and it's a goddamn raccoon on my damn back porch, so I put the silencer on and shot that little bastard. I knew that might have been wrong because I rob drug dealers, but shit it is what it is. I grabbed that little fucker and threw it into my neighbors' yard with that loud as barking dog. I went take a quick shower and hit up Lil Mike to let him know to meet me at the spot. I didn't want anymore problems because after what happened that last time, we pulled a caper.

Chapter 18

Head

Man, we finally got out the bitch and I'm not going back. These hoes gave us a court date. But, trust me, I won't be around to see that bitch. I've always wanted to go fuck around in California anyway, but I decided to pull a big ass lick and head west before I do. "Thank you for coming through for me and Unc. Alicia, you really came through for your cousin and Unc." She looked at me, staring, and said nigga, "This shit wasn't free," and proceeded to tell me that she took twenty bands for her trouble. Shit, I wasn't tripping because what I had in store for her wasn't going to compare to what she took. I told her to drop Unc off and I had something to holler about Alicia. So, we drop my uncle off and I told her to drive me to the crib on Forsythe that nobody knew about but Alicia, Unc, and I. We pulled up and hopped out and I looked around to see if we were followed and no one was in sight. I put the code in and turned the key, and, as I looked around, I saw everything was still in its place. I told Alicia to go make something to eat quickly. She rolled her damn eyes but proceeded to the kitchen. I went to take a quick shower and came back downstairs, and Alicia had it smelling good as fuck in that kitchen and she told me to hurry the fuck up and told her what's up. I got my grub on and told her that I'm going to have to kill her little boyfriend Lil Mike and his brother Josh. She looked at me and said "No the fuck you don't" and started saying all kind of bullshit. I let her finish and told her that he and his brother are the reason behind me and Unc going to jail. She screams at me saying I have the wrong man and I told her that bitch ass brother of his killed our niece and she starts crying. I hugged her and she started beating on my chest like she was mad at me. She was because when my brother got locked up, I was the one who was supposed to support and raise my niece like my own. Hell, she didn't have to tell me I fucked up, I knew that shit and it was killing me. So, I had to kill that nigga and take what's near and dear to him and that meant his mama and little brother. She looked at me and said,

"How do you know it was him though?"

"Alicia, stop being fucking dumb: I had cameras in that fucking trap house and I got everything on tape. These niggas thought I was stupid, so, I made them pay a ransom with money and I told them I burned all the tapes, but that was a lie. I kept one because I knew something would come of this. I've made a lot of money selling weight and you've made enough robbing the competition and it's time to start somewhere else. I need you to say your goodbye's and help me get this nigga off guard so you can help me kill him and take what is near and dear to him. I need to know if you have my back, Alicia. Now, tonight my biggest trap house is getting a load of my money and I have a bad feeling about tonight. I moved the location and three people knew about it. So, if something didn't go right, I was killing everybody that knew. Look Alicia, if something ever happens to me, my insurance papers are in my room under the baseboards. I left everything to you and our niece, but now she's gone, it's up to you to make this shit happen if something ever happens to me." She hugged me and said nothing would happen to me. She hugged me and left, and I was right about that night: I had a funny feeling. I went in my closet and grabbed two more 40 cals and headed out. I needed to get some pussy to calm a nigga's nerves, so I hit that bitch Trice up that I knew was fucking that nigga Josh up for some midday pussy. I hit her up and she said something about her and that nigga got into it or something like that. I didn't give a fuck: I was going to use that bitch to get to this nigga after I got the pussy and killed her also if I had to. The pussy was good though, so I didn't mind using her for what she had. The head game was top notch, so I hit Interstate 20 and picked the bitch up.

Chapter 19

Lil Mike

I got a call from Josh and he sounded like he was panicking, and I didn't like that shit. I tried to call my mama, but she wasn't answering and that wasn't like her. I decided to just check on her after I met Josh at the spot: we purchased off other nigga's hard work. I knew this bitch who worked at Chase and she did all my paperwork for me to get into the house. She introduced me to the real estate agent that I also fucked to get the house and the rest was history. I drove up to the crib and I heard Young Dolph blasting from the back of Josh's bedroom. I banged on the door and that nigga was in there smoking a blunt, staring into space like he was in deep thought about something he was about to tell me. I dapped him up and asked him what was so important, and he said he had some shit to tell me so I needed to sit-down so we could discuss the shit. I first asked him if he had heard from mama. He said that's part of the reason he wanted to talk to me. He said some shit went down with Brian and his mama, so he sent mama to go stay with Aunt Brenda for a few weeks in Vegas. I asked him why the fuck would he do that and not tell me, and he said every decision he makes he doesn't have to tell me. He was right as rain and I was so used to being his big brother that I didn't take the time to remember he was a grown ass man now. So, I shut the fuck up and listened. He then told me what that nigga did to Brian's mama. This nigga Head

52

had somebody to pull his dick out and piss on this old lady's shoes and I'm getting heated all over again because if they would've done this to my mama, I know I would've been ready to kill something. I asked him what he had in mind and he told me we needed to get rid of Head. I told him that I knew this nigga just got out of jail and he was coming for us. I shook my head because before my brother robbed the nigga, I heard about his way of handling shit in the street. He told me he knew where he was getting a drop and only a few niggas knew about it. I heard a loud bang coming from the bathroom and it's a nigga who's tied up and gagged trying to talk. I yelled at Josh and asked what the fuck and why the fuck was it a nigga in the bathroom in our crib that no one knew about. He said, "That's the nigga who pissed on Brian's mama shoes I was telling you about and that nigga gave up the location for tonight of the drop." Brian dropped him off a little while ago, so we've been hanging out. I often wondered if my little brother was a pathological killer, but it is what it is. So, he told me it's going down that night, and he's prepared to die for this shit.

Before I left, he looked at me and told me that he saw Alicia running out of Head's trap house that night and asked why the fuck would she be in a trap house late at night when she doesn't do drugs. I asked him why the fuck he's never told me that before, and at this time I asked him if he was sure it was her. He told me that the nigga informed him that Head is Alicia's cousin and I was fucking blew now for real. He told me to be ready at 10 PM and meet on Burg Jones Lane so we could get this nigga. I dapped him up and told him that I'm going to holler at him in a few. I got in the car and talked to myself all the way home. *Where the fuck did Alicia get all that money from? Was this bitch setting me up the whole time? Couldn't be though because I tried to talk to her that day in the mall. She never told me what she did. Let me call her and ask her some shit.*

Chapter 20

Alicia

As I sat here in the house, tripping over what's got to happen within the next few days, my phone rings and it's Lil Mike. I didn't want to answer because I got close to this dude and I had move on. I was in tears, knowing that I must go to California to get away. I wiped my face and put on my big girl panties and answered the phone all sexy and shit like was nothing wrong. I said, "Hey bae, where are you? I miss you." He said with that sexy ass baritone voice that he misses me too and that he needed me to answer a few questions. He said, "Bae, I never asked you how you got that big, nice ass apartment with no job," and he added, "Let me find out you a stripper at night," and laughed. I was getting big mad, but I played it cool and said I'm only stripping for you. That's about it. I told him to come throw some dollars this way. He laughed and then asked me on a serious note how I got the crib and the car I was driving, and he knew I didn't have a job. I didn't want to answer him, but I told him I had a close family in jail and when he passed away, he left it to me, and he said, "Oh okay; that's what's up." He then asked me if I knew a nigga named Head and I'm thinking *Oh shit, here we go*, but I knew I had to be quick on my feet to keep this nigga off balance. I pretended to get mad and say, "Yes, that bitch ass nigga is my cousin and I hate that he is. He's the black sheep of the family and always does wrong; do you know he let my niece get killed by some niggas that he doesn't even know? I cried and cried about this." I proceeded to tell him I went over there a few weeks ago because he said he had some money for me and he didn't want to pay so I left his trap house, man. "Wait, love, how do you know Head?"

"From around the way, you know, but someone told me they saw you the other day running out of his trap house and I forgot to ask you. That's it, boo. One more question, how do you feel about riding with me somewhere tonight?" I told him it's whatever and I'm down for anything and he knew that. As we hung up the phone, my mind went a hundred miles a minute and I told myself to call Head because this nigga knew and, just in case this nigga tried anything, to be ready. I always knew Head would be the downfall of the family, but he always seemed to bounce back from everything. Now, that part wasn't a lie. I thought what the fuck does this dude have up his sleeve and where the fuck did he want to take me. I was going to be in some a black sheep shirt, some Levi's and some J's that just came out with my baby 380 in my Fendi purse that I just got. If he wanted to get it popping, then we could. He really didn't know that I could be a killer if pushed. My niece didn't deserve all this shit. We wanted better for her and her friends. She was supposed to be the one who made it legally and not like us. She was a beautiful, young lady and had a lot going for her and, for her, I would die and that's on me.

Chapter 21

Head

As I made it to Trice's crib, I knew that nigga Josh was not there because they had a little fight or whatever. As I'm riding, my cousin Alicia hit me up and told me everything and I told her I have a plan that is going to end this shit. She asked me if it's something else that she needed to do and I told her, "Fuck it; go ride with the nigga and make sure you break that nigga off and keep him off balance for as long as you could. Shit could go down tonight, so be alert and make sure to erase all calls and texts to me because that nigga might want to go through your phone or something shit, I don't know." She told me that she would keep me posted. I made it to Trice's crib, and she told me to park in the back alley because it's too obvious with my big ass Escalade with forge's on it. So, I did what I was told and parked in the back. I hopped out with my two guns in my waist band and put the alarm on my shit. I made it in the crib and this bitch had candles lit with slow music going and I'm like, "I'm just here to fuck but it is what it is," and I just go along. She said, "Hey daddy, I missed you and gave me a peck on my lips." Now, usually, I don't kiss bitches, but this bitch's lips were so fucking soft, and that lip gloss was on just right. I love getting my dick sucked with that lip shit on because it drives a nigga crazy. I told her big fine ass I missed her too (which I kind of did, but her ass is annoying when I'm not there to break her off some money or some good dick.) She said she fucked with that nigga for security and I didn't understand that. These bitches don't love niggas no more like they used to: hell, these broads are more savage than some of these niggas. We kicked it on the couch for a minute doing small talk and all that bullshit until I told her that those thighs were looking good and I wanted to test that pussy and lips out. She told me we've been fucking for two years and I knew how every part of her tasted and felt and laughed. I told her she is right about that. Now, I don't ever eat broads, but, like I said, man, this chick had me gone, but she would never fucking know that shit. That's just how we rolled in my family. We will fuck you like we love you, but still be single at the same time. I could never see how someone could get married knowing this bitch was going to get half of your shit in the end. Like that nigga Drake say *Bitch, you weren't with me shooting in the gym.* Anyway, she said we needed to go upstairs because she wanted to ride my face and my dick anyway. She swished that big ass of hers upstairs and my dick got instantly hard all over again. She told me to get comfortable and to take off my clothes. I did what was asked of me because I didn't have that much time to get this pussy; hell, I had to go kill her nigga and his brother. She came out the bathroom and asked if I was ready big daddy and that pussy was so fucking pretty. I told her "fuck yea and bring that pussy to me and sit on my face," and that's exactly what she did. I laid back and let her ride my face like it was no tomorrow; shit, for some people, it's not going to be a tomorrow, so fuck it: I had to get me. She was smothering the fuck out of my face, but I didn't give a fuck at all. I'll breathe through my ears if necessary just so I can taste the pussy again and again. She busted again and told me she wanted to ride the dick and I threw her off my face to get on my dick. She slowly put it in and started rocking and it must have felt good to her because she told me when a bitch rides you, she tries to spell the word *coconut* on the dick and that would make them bust faster. So, I seen her mumble the letters *c o c o* and then she came: she was in a state of bliss when I thought I heard something coming up the stairs and she said, "Naw, don't move!" She was about to bust again and that's when the door flung open and I flung her off of me, and she started screaming. I got on the side of the bed and thank God my guns were by my shoes. The next thing I knew all the lights in the house went off.

Chapter 22

Josh

"Man, get rid of this nigga, Brian, and take him to Robinson Place and dump that nigga in front of that church before you turn in and say, *Lord, forgive me because I have sinned* and piss on that nigga's body like he did your mama." He asked what I was about to do and I told him I needed to go back to Trice's crib because I left one of my guns and she was mad at a nigga. I told her I wasn't coming back that night, so I figured she'd have an attitude when I showed up. I didn't give a fuck because she's my baby and fuck all these other bitches. I knew she had a nigga's back in the end. He dapped me up and told me to be ready that night so we could meet on Burg Jones Lane. I left on my bike, then I stopped by Valero's to pick up a few cigars to celebrate after we hit this nigga Head and got his cash. I made it to Trice's crib, but I had a fucked up feeling in my stomach and I couldn't shake the shit to be honest. I thought to myself that I was just tripping and would be straight after I laid low in Vegas with mom. I put the key in and I swear I heard moaning like she was getting some dick, but she told me that she sometimes plays with her wand dildo that she got from the X-Mart store, but she threw me off this time when she said out loud that she was almost there and be still, so I took out my fucking gun and went upstairs. I peeked through the door and saw this bitch riding a nigga. I couldn't believe it that this bitch had the nerve to have a nigga up in the bitch I paid the bills for, fucking him. I busted in that bitch blasting and I hit Trice once in the arm, although I was aiming for that nigga. I would've handled her ass later, but somehow that nigga landed on the side of the bed and starting shooting at my fucking feet. All I heard was that nigga saying, "Come on in here, fuck nigga, and get this smoke. You thought they stopped making straps after they made yours, pussy nigga?" He shot Trice twice, and I heard the screaming stop. I was hella mad now: this bitch nigga done killed my broad. I yelled that I was going to kill this motherfucka for fucking my bitch and killing her. He yells, "Fuck that bitch and you nigga: I'm going to kill you and your fucking brother, bitch."

I yelled back, "Bitch, you must got nine lives because you going to die here tonight." I heard this nigga moving as if he was putting on his clothes, so I decided to make my move and started shooting, but that nigga was not in the room. I checked the bathroom and that nigga wasn't there. I looked out the window and I saw that damn Escalade pulling off. This bitch ass nigga jumped out the window and I was mad as fuck because he knew I was after him. I started to call the police for Trice, but, hell, she was gone, and there was nothing I could do for her now. I kissed her on the lips and told her goodbye. I gathered all my shit and my cash I had stashed in her closet and got my guns and left. I picked up all the shell casings just in case of anything. I got on the phone with Lil Mike and told him what happened, and he was beyond pissed now. I told him to drop everything because it's about to go down. My next call was to Brian and the crew and they were so heated that them niggas were ready to go. I told him to not do shit until we got there and asked if he understood me. I hopped on my bike and rode out.

Chapter 23

Head

That bitch nigga thought he was going to kill me right then, I thought to myself *Nigga, I'm like an old cockroach: I'm hard to kill in this bitch.* I'm hyped at this point, so I called my hitters and told them what happened, and they are some live wires, so I knew them niggas were ready. I was willing to die behind my name and what was mine. I guess he thought I wasn't going to kill that bitch. She must have told him I was there because how did that bitch ass nigga knew I was there. So, what I did was justified to the fullest, and I really liked that bitch. Oh well, it is what it is.

As I drove to my duck off spot, I saw the lights behind me and I started to pull over and thought to myself *Fuck, I'm sweating, got blood on me, and got these two pistols in the front seat. Me getting pulled over can't be a coincidence.* I pulled over and thought: *Here it is I'm going to jail behind some stupid shit as if I didn't just kill a whole fucking person.* As I pulled over, he kept driving past me and I say to myself: *Thank you God, even though after all the shit I've done in my life, He doesn't even hear me or see me anymore.* I got it that *thou shalt not kill or steal or sell drugs* like I've done, but sometimes you must do what you have to in order to survive. I pulled off slowly because that was a fucking close call indeed, and I needed to kill this nigga before going to California. Now, I knew there were only three people who knew about the drop that night and one was not answering the phone, which was the first red flag. So, I kept calling him and still no answer and, by that time, I'm thinking that nigga is deep in some pussy or he is doing some underhanded shit. I tried to give him the benefit of the doubt, but he had three hours to get back at me or I'd send them goons after him. I called Alicia to see if she was still keeping that nigga close because it was going down that night and to tell her that bitch ass nigga brother came after me and almost took me out, but I didn't let him do a shit. I did manage to kill his bitch though and all I heard next was silence because I knew she was cool with that broad, but I didn't give a fuck really. "Alicia, look this is what's going to happen, man, go out with the nigga tonight and just play everything off just right. If you can get that nigga back to your crib, text me when your there, I want that mother fucker dead! You hear me, fucking *dead*." Now, I knew I could count on her to do what's best for our family. I made it to the house to wipe this bitch's blood off me and to get ready for that night. I already paid them little niggas, so I knew it was up there when we got there. I prayed and hoped those niggas were ready to die because some of them would not make it back. *You know how that shit is* I told myself as I got ready. I rolled up a blunt and took a deep pull off that bitch and I knew God didn't fuck with me like that, but I prayed anyway and asked Him if He could forgive me for all the wrong I've done to others just to make a quick dollar or two. I also asked Him to watch over my cousin and uncle because they were literally all I had left in this world. I also asked him to watch over me as I went to do this so I could go to California and get my next chapter in life started. I got up off my knees and said *Thank you, Jesus* and made a few more phone calls. It was about to go down.

Chapter 24

Lil Mike

I took Alicia out to a few places before I knew I had to kill her, and I just wanted to get this one last time before I went to Vegas and kicked it with my people for a little while. I arrived at her place so we could go out to eat. I told her to be ready because I made reservations and we could not be late to the exclusive restaurant. I picked her up in a rental car I got a meth head to rent for me because I needed to kill her in this car and burn the body. I knew that was fucked up, but there couldn't be any witnesses and I had to make sure all my ducks were lined up in a row so I could shoot them bitches down. She was looking so fucking good and I can't lie, it was going to hurt me to kill her, but it is what it is. I checked under my seat to see if the strap was still under there. I opened the door for her so I would seem like the perfect gentleman and nothing seemed off. She was all smiles, and I loved it. We were in the car flirting and holding hands and everything was fine. I put my phone on airplane mode because I didn't want any interruptions. We made it to the restaurant, and the atmosphere was amazing: we had drinks with a bomb ass conversation. She was even trying to let me know she was ready to fuck me when we left. We were full and tipsy, and she told me she needed to use the bathroom and when she was gone, I looked at my phone and I had five missed calls from mama and twelve missed calls from Josh. I told my-self I would just have to hold on for a little while longer. I saw her coming back from the bathroom and she was still tipsy, I could see, so I paid the check and we dipped. As the valet pulled the car around, she looked at me and asked if I could see her in my future. I looked at her and said, "Hell yes, I do and was wondering if we could take this to the next level," even though I knew I was about to kill her in just a few minutes. Now she knew I loved head, and it's nothing like road head. She looked straight ahead and pulled my dick out of my pants and started jacking him off. I said, "Let's take this to Magnolia Park so you can suck him properly." She just giggled and bit her bottom lip and told me to let the seat back. She started going in on my dick and I loved every minute of it, but as soon as I came, I was going to blow her fucking brains out just like she did mine. She was sucking, slurping, slobbering all over him and I felt myself about to bust and I did and she swallowed every fucking drop. As I told her to keep going, I reached under the seat and put the gun to her head while her eyes were closed, sucking my dick, I blew her fucking brains out. Blood was everywhere and I felt bad for her. At the same time, I didn't because of her cousin. She probably didn't deserve to die, but I had to or at least that's what I told my-self. She was lying there with blood just pouring out like lava out of a volcano. I had to drive with her dead in my car so I could burn that bitch up. I drove her to this abandoned warehouse where I left some clothes and my car there. I parked and hopped out the car. I changed clothes and put gas all over her body and all over the rental car. Hell, it's not in my name, so fuck it. I sat there and watched her burn and I asked the Man upstairs for forgiveness. Hell, I know that He probably won't do it, but I hope He understood that, for my sake. I left her body there and I drove away like she was nothing. It's nothing else to say about it, but I drove to the crib and tried to relax and take a shower. I still wanted to get out of those clothes and make sure I was straight for that night because I would probably go to Vegas straight after we killed this nigga. Shit, let me call this nigga Josh back after he blew my damn phone up all damn night.

"What's up, brah?"

"What's going on?" He told me what happened at Trice's crib and I'm like, *What the fuck is wrong with this dude.* So, he's been fucking Trice for a while and you think it's been a setup the entire time. "Is that what you're telling me, Josh?" He proceeded to say he doesn't know, and he goes silent for a minute. I know my brother and I knew he is in deep thought. I asked him what he did with her body and his shit he had in that girl's house he stayed at most nights. That was his main chick, so I knew he was hurting, but I couldn't do anything about that. I told him we needed to talk about something anyway. "I'll come and get you so we can go back and burn her body, bro." He agreed and we hung up. I looked at the house one more time because I wouldn't be back for a while after the caper. I hopped in my car and rode out to Josh and I saw him on the curb on the cell phone talking to Brian. I dapped both them up and I told him that's some fucked up shit about his mama, but we got that motherfucker, so we're going to be straight.

"Look let me, holla at my brother real quick and we can go." He shook his head and proceeded to walk off and I just looked at Josh. "I didn't want to tell you over the phone, but I just killed Alicia, man." He didn't say anything; he just looked at me and said, "Nigga, you had to do what you had to do, right?

I said, "Of course, I did, and I would do it again if it meant protecting you and my family, brah." He hugged me and told B to come on so we could get this nigga, Head. So, we rode off and I looked at Josh and said, "This nigga really tried to kill you, brah, then he just shot Trice like that and got away."

He said, "That's what I said, didn't I?"

I said, "Chill, baby bro. I'm just getting the facts straight," then he said, "Nigga, let's just get on Burg Jones Lane so we can kill this nigga."

Chapter 25

Head

We and a few of my little goons were on Burg Jones Lane, a spot only we knew about. I had four little niggas at the front entrance if they were just talking and shooting the shit, but they were actually good. Shooter and I also placed four on the back of the warehouse, so if anyone else besides that white Wal-Mart 18-wheeler pulled up, then it was lights out for anyone else. Now, I know what you might be thinking: why would I get a Wal-Mart 18-wheeler truck involved with some shit I'm doing illegally? Those trucks are hella cheap to a nigga like me and not suspicious about dropping off something to a warehouse. I did my research, and we ran this bitch about 20 times, so I kept doing it. I had Wal-Mart supplies in the back of the truck just in case the truck got pulled over and my bricks wrapped inside of furniture and a few refrigerators. I wouldn't get caught with all that product and money I had hidden in secret departments throughout the truck. Hell, after this, I was giving the game up to my lil' homey who's been holding me down and I would be out to California with my cousin Alicia. She hadn't been answering her phone, so I assumed she was still out with that bitch ass nigga. He would be gone soon, so I didn't know what she was going to do. Plus, I had a close fucking call that day and I needed a fresh start. All I wanted was my money and the shipment to be sold, and, hell, I already had buyers for it. It just needed to it to be broken down and distributed all throughout the south. I called one of my workers to get the forklift and get all that other bullshit like TVs and other shit out the back of it so I could get to the other side. I told everybody but me, my partner, and the forklift driver to stay inside and I told them they could go to the crib. I paid them and I left. I got into the office and I saw niggas jumping out the back of the truck and instantly killing my forklift driver and my partner and shot out the window to my office. These niggas were shooting hard and now I'm wondering why the fuck I told them niggas to go home. I usually don't trust nobody with counting my product because I do it myself, but that was looking like a mistake I made and it was too late for a nigga. I heard footsteps coming into my office and I left my guns in the car because all these niggas were there. I found a wrench and I was hiding behind a clothes rack. I knew I was about to die, so I asked God to save me, but He didn't hear my prayers because, when I opened my eyes, it was that bitch ass nigga Josh and I told him: *Bitch, I won't beg for my life: do what you have to.* He said, "I'm not going to kill you, my man," then said, "Sike," and I felt the bullet in my shoulder sting like a bitch, but I didn't cry: I took that shit like a fucking gansta that I am. Live by the gun and die by that bitch. I said nigga, "Just kill me already; what the fuck are you waiting for?" He shot me in the leg and said, "Bitch nigga, don't rush me. I'll kill you slowly," and then Brian walked in, and I knew it was over then. He looked at Josh and asked, "Why isn't that nigga dead yet?" and I said, "Because he is a hoe like you, bitch, made fuck boy." He pointed the gun, and everything goes black.

Chapter 26

Lil Mike

I guess I had to trust my brother more often and realize that he is not a little boy anymore. I must step back and realize that he is not that little dude I used to walk to the bus stop. From that day forward, I wouldn't say anything out the way to my brother and just let him do him. We were all ready to go to Vegas when he said, "Let's go to Trice's grave because I want to say a few words before we leave this bitch for a little while."

I said, "Are you sure about that because of what happened that night we went back to burn the house down that she was still in dead?" As we approached the house, we saw nothing, but red and blue lights filled the street with yellow tape and coroners' vans on the scene. We looked at each other and knew it was too late to burn the body. The old lady across the street said that she heard shooting and saw a big Escalade drive off. I'm thinking, *I hope they didn't see my brother's bike and wouldn't identify him.* As we looked at each other, the coroner is bringing out her body and that nigga shed a tear and I understood completely because I just killed my bitch Alicia. So, we drove off and he told me the dude he killed earlier told him all of Head's plans and the only way to get Head was to put some niggas in the back on the Walmart truck and when he got his money out, jump out, and light his ass up and that shit worked to perfection. We hit that nigga hard, especially when I gave the go ahead. I had a hitter outside, and he told me all his goons were leaving. He then told Josh he counts all the drugs himself and that's exactly what Head was doing. He was in his office when we started busting at him. I mean, this was too easy. I should have trusted my brother with this plan, and I'm glad I did. We got all his money from the truck and we took it back to Brian's crib. We laid low there for a few weeks until this blew over. So, we stepped out of the car so Josh could say his goodbyes to Trice. We walked up to the grave and as we all said goodbye, I heard a voice say: *It's all right, son. Who was she to you?* and I looked back and this nigga the spitting image of me and I said, "Pops?" It was that nigga Big Mike looking like me, but with a few more scars. I knew this was about to get crazy and I was ready for the ride.

Chapter 27

Big Mike

As I stared at my son Lil Mike, he was staring back with a look of disgust at me. I completely understood, and I would've done the same thing after not seeing my pops for seven years. I knew he had a lot of questions and I planned on answering them all in due time. I was just hoping that the grave that my sons were staring at was not their mother. I loved my sons' mother and tried to do right by her on so many occasions. I had a lot of kids allegedly, and I really was a rolling stone. When I met the boy's mother, I was a senior in high school. I was the star outside linebacker, and I was a hell of a basketball player as well. She was a cheerleader and you know how that goes in high school. The jocks go after the prettiest cheerleader. I walked up to her one day and smiled; I got the smile back, and I asked her for her number. After that, we were inseparable, and I loved every minute. Now, I've always had different girls in different area codes way before Ludacris. The real trouble started when we both graduated from high school. I went to a Division 1 school because of football and she went to a HBCU called Grambling University. I loved Grambling's culture though, and that band was unmatched, even though people say Southern is way better, but that's a story for another time. When I went to college, I nearly lost my mind because the women were better all the way around. I wasn't dealing with little girls anymore and I knew it. This is when the problems started. She would call and I would say I was busy, knowing I was with another girl. The boys' mother caught me a few times with other girls, but I always got her back. We fell out of touch for a while. I thought I had all the answers until that one day on the field where I blew out my knee. I thought I would be back on the field in no time. They didn't have all the technology that they have now. I didn't have the opportunities that these kids have. I was just ready to go to the league, and that was my goal. After I blew out my knee, I was never the same. After my scholarship fell through, I was on academic probation and I never worked because I was the star athlete. Man, I dropped out and had to go back home and, hell yes, it embarrassed me because I didn't make it to the league. So, I had to swallow my pride and go back home. The thing about going home after not making it is the people who're looking at you like *Damn, you messed up your life*. I guess it was just karma on my part and I thought the weight of the world was on my shoulders at that time. I did run back into their mother at the club one night and I hugged her tight. She explained to me that she had a new boyfriend, but I really didn't give a damn because I needed her. I did get her number and we started kicking it again. I told her to leave her boyfriend for me and I would do what I could to take care of her. At this time, I already had two other kids allegedly by two women around town. The boys' mother wanted kids of her own, so we planned Lil Mike and had him. He was the spitting image of me when he was born, and I was proud as hell. Even though I had two allegedly kids, their mothers wouldn't let me see them because I was with Lil Mike's mama. Baby mama drama is a real thing: trust me, I know it. We were doing good at that time and then came Joshua. He was my youngest son because I fucked around and cheated on their mother and had another child with another woman. She flipped out, but she kept taking me back time after time. Until this day, I have no idea why she kept taking me back. I know for a fact: if I would've seen her cheating on me, I wouldn't have taken her back. We were doing good at first, but I just couldn't stop cheating and drinking. I had a real problem, but I'm a man and I can admit when I'm wrong. A woman scorned is something serious because, as the boys grew up, I couldn't find a job, so I started selling weight and it came naturally to me. Before I knew It, I had the whole northside and southside sewed up. They belonged to me and I had them blocks popping. Then one night, I was going to pick up three kilos from my plug Rodriguez. The transaction went smooth as usual and I went by my way. As I was driving down South Third Street, I saw them red and blue lights pop on from behind me. I was nervous as hell because I had three kilos in the trunk, and I knew this would be the end of me. Especially with these racist as cops. They were just looking for a black man to act up so they could have a reason to pull their state issued strap and shoot the fuck out of them. I pulled over and tried not to sweat or look nervous. I knew I wasn't speeding, so it had to be the blue Mercedes Benz that I was in with heavy tint. Looking back at it, I guess I could've been in a more lowkey car. But why do I have to ride in a car that is not up to my standards? I was making money hand over fist with this weight I was moving. He pulled me over and told me to roll the fucking window down with his flashlight almost breaking my fucking window. I'm heated at this point, but what the fuck can I do about it? He told me to get out the car and I asked him what I did, trying to keep my composure, but this fucking cop was pulling and yanking all on me. He told me to interlock my fingers behind my head. He read me my rights and, at this point, I asked what the fuck I did. He told me to shut the fuck up and put me in the back of the police car. He checked my fucking trunk and knew exactly where the dope was. I had it in a secret compartment in the trunk, so I knew this bastard knew way more than he was supposed to. At this point, another squad car pulled up and he comes to my side and told me I fucked up and it's a way for me to get out of this mess I'm in. I told him from the jump I didn't know what the fuck he was talking about and I was being set up. He looked at me and told me to not fucking lie to him. He said I was looking at a lot of time or I could go home right now and tell them where Rodriguez's meeting spot is at. I looked at him and asked who the fuck that was. He said to the other officer to take me downtown because I am facing sixty-five years and that's on me. I said, "Fuck you; I'm not giving you shit." So, they locked my black ass up with the quickness. I was making all that money, so busy worried about shining and getting money, that I didn't get a fucking lawyer that I could count on. Basically put: I was really fucked royally with no plan on getting on and, two days after I didn't show up, somebody was already trying to steal my fucking blocks. I was thinking to myself, *I'm not going to even tell nobody where I'm at.* I told the boys' mama that I was going out for milk and that's why I kept it like that because they didn't know what I did. I would take that secret to myself and wouldn't tell anybody. I was facing one hundred years if convicted and I couldn't do that time; therefore, I had to become a confidential informant. I know that shit sounds like a snitch, but I had to do what the fuck I had to. I would serve six and a half years as a confidential informant. I was locked up with killers, rapists, extortionists, and everybody else. My size and my demeanor is what kept me out of a lot of shit. I have snitched on three drug dealers in jail and, I hate to admit the shit but, yes: I did it to cut my time and make me get out of jail faster. I hated fucking jail, but you couldn't tell by the way I carried myself. That is why I was there standing at the grave sight looking at my boy. The state wanted me to turn on my own fucking son and I told them that I would, but I would never tell on them. I just told them that shit to get me out of jail. I could never tell Lil Mike and Josh this shit, so I had to tread lightly on how I approached this. I hated being a snitch, but they said my son killed some lady and they needed fucking proof. We will see how this turns out, won't we?

Chapter 28

Lil Mike

I can't believe this bastard had the audacity to come to that fucking grave site after all these years and we don't know where this bitch made fool has been. I looked over at Josh and he was stunned, just like me. We looked at each other for a minute and we are speechless and didn't know what to say. So, he said, "I guess we are putting Vegas on hold until we get some more shit straight." I looked Big Mike dead in the eyes and told him he could've stayed gone because we did not fucking need him then and we don't need his bitch ass now. Josh told me to hold on and hear this nigga out. I was not trying to hear anything out of his fucking mouth. I said we must go to Vegas and check on mama and I looked over at Big Mike and he smiled as I talked about my mama. "What the fuck are you smiling about?" as he looked at me and said, "Man, I miss your mama."

I said, "Bitch ass nigga: if you even thinking you even getting close to my mama again, you are a fucking fool." Just as I was about to give this nigga some more of my mind, I saw red and blue lights surrounding us. I looked at Josh and asked if he is holding his strap, and he said no. I didn't have mine so they couldn't have been there for us. Just as I said that, six police came up to me and told us to freeze, put our hands on our head, and another one said for us to get on the ground. I asked, "Which one do you want me to do: freeze or get on the fucking ground?" Suddenly, three enormously buff assholes come tackle me to the ground and put the handcuffs on me. He read me my rights. But one officer looked at Big Mike and gave him a wink. I didn't think anything of it. These fucking cops told me this was about the murder of Alicia Bynum and I immediately shut the fuck up until I could talk to my lawyer. The cop noticed that I said nothing else because I would not snitch on myself. That is a big ass no-no because I fucking hate snitches. I mean, I despise the fuckers because, most likely when you were in that position, you knew the risk, so why snitch on the next man? Especially family. I would rather die in a cell than rat on my family. A million things are running though my mind because I hoped they didn't have any actual evidence on me about Alicia's murder because I wiped everything clean and I burned her body so that shouldn't be the case. I didn't know what they could have on me. On top of that, "Big Mike is back and from where though?" I always asked myself what I would do to this nigga if I ever seen him again, and before I could say what I wanted to, these fucking police show up. I can't go to Vegas right now with all this shit going on. I knew my mama would flip out when she found out that I was in jail accused of killing the girl she said was right for me and she liked. That was a lengthy ride to jail and a quiet one. The police didn't say a damn word to me, and I liked it like that because I needed time to think, anyway. They took me inside and took my fingerprints and I went through the process of going to jail but I had a feeling that I wouldn't be out of that bitch soon. I just hoped Josh was not about to do something stupid while I was in jail0. I needed him to get away to Vegas because he killed Head and I needed him to get the fuck from around there. I needed a phone to contact him and tell him to leave right fucking now. I didn't want him in that bitch no more than I wanted to be in there. I hoped Josh didn't fall for whatever that nigga Big Mike was back for. Fuck, I had to get my hands on a phone inside that bitch, but I had to watch my back because I robbed a couple of niggas that was in that bitch, so I didn't know how that shit was about to turn out.

Chapter 29

Josh

Man, this couldn't be happening when we were supposed to be on a plane headed to Vegas. I blamed myself because I wanted to go to the gravesite to say my goodbyes to Trice, but now it's looking like that got cut short. Damn, my father, Big Mike, was back and it was bothering me because I didn't know what to say about all this shit. I remember this nigga, but I didn't remember him like that. I looked up to Lil Mike because he was always there for a nigga through it all. I got jumped one day from these niggas from the westside of town and I was just over there to get some ass and I got jumped. I told my big brother, and he went over there and whipped up on three dudes and I loved that shit. It was like he was giving them fuckers lessons because he was telling them a little knowledge as he beat them up. For instance, one boy he beat up was telling him you don't beat on another man's brother because of the brother's keeper rule. I was like that's what's up then and he beat his ass. I didn't have any dad memories, so I kept that nigga at a fucking distance until I got my brother out. I needed to hold off on telling mom because she was loving Vegas and I didn't want to rain on her parade. I needed to ask her a lot about this nigga Big Mike though and how I should proceed with this nigga. She would have a lot of questions about him. I just didn't have the time to answer. He told me to come and give him a hug like I was tiny kid. I hesitated at first, but I told him it was nice to see him. He told me that later if we had time, we could chop it up like men and discuss getting whatever trouble my brother was in fixed in a hurry. I just shook my head and agreed with all that bullshit he was talking about. If it's one thing Lil Mike taught me, it's that take a man at face value. Look in his eyes when he's speaking to see if you can find out if he's lying or not. I had a funny feeling about this dude, but I let it go. He asked if I needed a ride to the precinct and I told him no because I wanted to be alone and I would get with him tomorrow. He asked for my phone so I could get in touch with him; I obliged and gave him my phone. I dapped him up and told him to be safe out here in these streets.

Chapter 30

Big Mike

Man, it was good seeing my boys and even better hugging Josh. Even though it was short-lived, I enjoyed looking in their eyes, but why the fuck did Detective Brown wink at me? What the fuck was that and I was heated because they were supposed to get him when I wasn't around. I knew my son was way smarter than that and he was able to put two and two together because I know I would. I had no words about it and I just wanted to make sure all this shit went away. The fucking cops told me what they had on Lil Mike and I was devastated because of the conviction rate on criminals and especially black criminals. Josh mentioned something about going to Vegas and, when I talked to him the next day, I hoped he'd tell me more about his mama because I missed her dearly. When I was locked up, all I could do is think about her smile and how we used to be. I was fifty-one years old, but my sex drive was still on point. I intended on using this fucker soon because I hadn't had no pussy in seven years. I was tired of beating my dick every night on the bottom bunk of a nigga who could hear me when I fucking bust. I needed some ass and that night was the perfect night to do it. I went to the local strip club to see what was shaking with these new and improved females. I walked in and grabbed me a little table in the back: I just wanted to see what was up for the night. A little petite thang came to my table and asked me what I wanted to drink. I told her a Hennessy and two Bud Lights so she wouldn't have to keep coming back. She was sexy to be so little, but that wasn't what I was looking for. I love a female with glasses and that damn lip gloss that's shiny. That does something to me, so when she sucks on me, I can see it while she tries to swallow this rod. I mean, don't let the old age fool you. Fifty-one is the new thirty-one, and he still got power in him. I will let him out on a bitch, no doubt about that. That night, I planned on doing just that to somebody's daughter. The deejay announced the next girl coming to the stage goes by the name of Channel, so all the cheap bastards and punk ass ballers needed to fill her Chanel purse. She came on the stage with that song "Rake It Up" by Yo Gotti. She did her damn thing up there on the fucking stage. She was thicker than gumbo and I love me some gumbo: we caught eyes for a minute. I walked up to the stage and threw a hundred dollars in singles and she liked that shit. I told her to holler at me when she was done with her set. She did just that and came over to me real slow like and I loved every bit of it. I told her to bring me some more drinks and she said she was going to order her some as well. I told her to do her and we had a fire conversation about everything and nothing at the same time. I just wanted to fuck, and she knew that shit from the jump. We talked and she told me her stage name again, and I asked what her real name was. She said Raven and I said like the bird as she shook her head yeah. Then a look of sadness came over her and I started to ask what's wrong, but she just asked if I wanted a dance or to fuck her. I always keep it real and told her I wanted a dance right now, but I did want to fuck her later. She told me I looked familiar like someone she knew, but it couldn't be because her father is dead. I agreed like I was interested in what she was talking about and told her after she got off to come to my suite to chill with me. I told her I was willing to pay a grand just for one night, but whispered to her after she got this dick, she's going to want to pay me. She said if it's worth it then I could get the pussy all the time and walked to get her things and we left. I said to myself, *I'm 'bout to beat this pussy up like the old days, but, damn, I don't have any more condoms.* They say never trust a stripper's condom, so I said fuck it and I would just pull out and make her suck it for this grand I was going to give her. She better had appreciated what I was giving her: I was already paying for the pussy and the room. The least she could do was swallow my damn children. We got back to the room and suddenly, she was actin' shy like a little kid. I told her, "Please don't be shy now because I just seen every part of you at the strip club." She said once again that I looked so familiar and she couldn't place a finger on it. So, I told her to come over and let me place a finger on her. I know it was corny, but I haven't had any pussy in a while and it was time to get to the business. Just as she was putting her head in my lap, I started coughing and coughing and coughing bad. Blood came out my mouth and my nose. She got freaked out a little by it and I could tell she was wondering what was up with me. I couldn't stop coughing for shit and my chest was hurting and I couldn't hardly breathe. I just asked her could we do this another time because I wasn't doing so good. I told her she could keep the money for her trouble and to get at me another day. She took the money and promised to call in a few days. We said our goodbyes and she left without looking back. At this point, I was mad at myself for trying to hide my secret from the world. I had stage four lung cancer and the doctors gave me twelve months to live. That is one of the biggest reasons I decided to be a confidential informant. The feds that I was working with decided I could do better on the outside than on the inside of a prison cell. I hated myself for even letting me get to that point. I never believed the doctor knew what she was talking about until I got a second opinion and she gave even more bad news. The cancer spread and I didn't have that long to live so they let me out with the condition that I would get close to my sons and to put them behind bars for murders and selling drugs. Even though they didn't sell drugs right off the bat. They just robbed the drug dealers and sold their products that they stole. If I didn't have cancer inside of me, I would've never taken the deal and that's on my life. It just spread so fast that I didn't have time to think about anything else but my family and how I could help them out as much as possible for my untimely demise. I just laid back on the hotel bed and slept as long as I could. The next day Josh and I would chop it up and make a connection.

Chapter 31

Raven

When I left the hotel that night, I had a funny feeling in the pit of my stomach. I couldn't figure out who that guy looked like until I got sober. He looked just like that bastard Lil Mike that I fucking despised with everything inside of me. I hated Lil Mike and I hoped and prayed he got everything he deserved for my best friend Alicia's sake. Alicia was truly my best friend and sister to the end. For her to be burned up the way she was, it was a travesty. The autopsy revealed her cause of death was a bullet to the fucking head. We were devastated when we heard the news. Then they found her cousin Head dead in a fucking warehouse like a fucking dog in the street. I think I cried for ten days straight. I'm the one who called the police on that bitch ass Lil Mike. What he doesn't know is: that night they went out the same day as her death. She called me in the restaurant's bathroom because she had a funny feeling about that night anyway. She called me and said if anything happens to her, her papers to her apartment and her other valuables were in her apartment under a baseboard under her bed. I don't know why she picked that spot, but I didn't pay it any mind because I thought Lil Mike loved my damn friend. She also said she had to cut him off after that night and kept saying that she was with Lil Mike if anything happened to her. I always kept that in the back of my mind. I was in a deep sleep when I received a phone call from the police asking me if I knew *Alicia* and I said yes. They asked if I could come down to the station and answer a few questions and that I did. When I got there, I asked if they had found my friend because I couldn't get in touch with her for a few days. They said my name was listed on a wallet found in a car that was barely legible to read, but they made out my name and number. I started to cry immediately because I felt as if my life was about to come to a crashing halt and it did. They identified her by her teeth and they wanted to ask me when was the last time I spoke to Alicia. I told them a few days ago, and she was out to eat with her boyfriend and one other thing she sounded like she was scared for her life with this guy. I told him Lil Mike's name, address, brother's address, mother's house, and everything under the sun. I stated that he was not a pleasant guy to my friend, and I kind of lied, but I knew he was the one who killed her and, somehow, he had something to do with Head's death also. "Alicia was my best friend," I told the police officer. They asked where his hangout spots were and asked me "Were I involved in illegal activities with them?" I said hell no and I meant that because I wasn't involved. I mean, he did take Alicia on a few robberies, but I wouldn't forgive myself if I turned into a snitch. I was always taught to hate snitches because they would tell on their own mothers. I just had no time for it. After giving them Lil Mike's information, I did not feel like what I did was snitching because I knew he did it. The officers told me that they would contact me if they had any other questions. That was the longest ride home that I took. I cried all in traffic because it hit me that I really lost my best friend to the same streets that we hustled on. It hurt me to my heart knowing that night I wouldn't ever see or hear from my best friend again. I decided to hit the guy up from the other night because he had me intrigued until he started coughing bad and bleeding. That kind of shocked me because he was a handsome man for an older guy. I just hoped he didn't have anything like AIDS or something like that because I couldn't take more bad news. He did have a big dick though and I wanted some of it; hell, I needed some of it at this point. I might as well have milked this old man for everything he had. He said his name was Antonio which is weird for some reason because all the *Antonio's* that I knew were way younger than he was. Instead, I decided to smoke a blunt and watch Netflix . I figured the dick would still be there tomorrow and I needed a good night's rest if I was going to keep up with that bitch Lil Mike's case.

Chapter 32

Josh

You have a collect call from Ouachita Correctional Center from **Michael Beasly,** *do you accept the call?* "Yes, I accept the call, so put him through." I hadn't talked to my brother in about five days and I was getting worried. I talked to his lawyer, and it wasn't good news what they had against my brother. The lawyer told me there was a shell casing with Lil Mike's print on it in a burnt-up car with Alicia's body inside, and they *had him dead to rights.* Whatever the fuck that means: I just knew it didn't sound fucking good, and I just didn't want to let my brother know that I was panicking the fuck out. I was wondering though if the car was burnt, how the fuck was a shell not burnt in a car that was completely burned to a crisp. It made little sense, so I just held my worries to myself because I had to do some more digging. He said, "What's up, lil bro? Are you holding it down out there while I'm on vacation?" he laughed, but I knew he was worried because I know my fucking brother. I told him we were good, and I didn't tell mama about anything because she worried a lot. I just told her we would be in Vegas soon, and I sent her some more money to hold her over. He asserted, "This jail shit won't be nothing, man, and I will be out soon." He asked if I talked to his lawyer and I told him I'd write it down what he told me and he got quiet. I asked if Lil Mike was there, and he said faintly that he didn't want to say anything else on the phone. I told him his lawyer would be up there soon and I paid up in full. *You have one-minute left on the call,* the operator says, and I told him, "Big bro, I know you got to go, so I love you man and keep your head up in there." He said he loves me back and to stay safe and one more thing: to not get close to that nigga Big Mike because he had a bad feeling about the nigga. I hung up, and I knew he was tripping in that bitch and I needed him to keep his head up. Why did he keep telling me to stay away from Big Mike? I genuinely wanted to get to know the nigga and see where the fuck he has been and why he came back now. I will always have my guard up on that, but I had questions about all that shit because I honestly was about to lose my fucking mind. I needed a blunt and a good nut to help me clear my mind. Even though it was no time for that because I heard a nigga was looking for me in these streets and I had to figure it out who the fuck it was, I felt like I was being followed, so I called Brian to call the guys and follow the person who was following me. They said that he was on it and I believed him. That was my dude and I trusted him with my life, and he trusted me. I picked up the phone and called Big Mike to meet him and to have a chat.

Chapter 33

Big Mike

When my son called me, I was in the shower, so I didn't answer the first time. I called him back and asked what was going on. He told me he needed to talk to me, and he needed answers about a few things. I told him, "Whatever you need to know, I'm here for you and your brother." I gave him the address to the hotel I was at and told him to meet me at the bar in about 30 minutes. That would give me time to tell him everything that was on my mind except me being a confidential informant. I got ready, walked downstairs and went sit at the hotel bar to have a drink. Even though I had stage four cancer, I was not supposed to be drinking. I figured my time here was short and why couldn't I have a drink with my son? I waited for about an hour and he showed up with four goons around him like he was kin to the Obamas or something. I asked if we could talk without all the bodyguards. I told him." I'm an old man, so what will happen here at this bar with these hotel cameras?" He thought about it and pointed to them to leave. He said, "I'm going to cut to the point: where the fuck have you been? Do you know how many nights we heard mama cry for you and Lil Mike, even though he would never admit to it. They loved you, man, and I was young, but you hurt them." I really apologized for everything, and he said to me that my apology was not enough. I could tell that Josh was hurt that I left also, but he didn't want to say it. I get that though and he's a man now, so I must be truthful about everything.

"Look, I'm going to tell you everything from the beginning to the end and you can take it for face value, or you can believe what I'm about to tell you. I was selling dope and I know you didn't know that I got caught up with the wrong people. I was locked up the whole time and I couldn't face your mother again because I told her I wouldn't fuck up again. I was ashamed, so I did my time like a man and never told you. I left your mama some money if something ever happened to me, but she never knew what happened to me. I truly am sorry about that and if I could take it back, I swear I would." He was just looking at me and I didn't know what he was thinking, and it's kind of scary how much he looked like his mother. He finally spoke and said, "Get the fuck out of here with that bullshit," and I told him this is the God's truth and I wouldn't lie to him.

"I also have something else to tell you about me; it will be a shocker, or you might not give a fuck, but I must tell you, son. I have stage four cancer," and I showed him the papers and some of my pills. He said the shit was too much for him to handle. He also asked how the fuck I got out of jail then and why would I come back in their lives just to inform them that I was going to fucking die in a year.

"This shit is just too much for me with all this shit going on. I have to tell Lil Mike. Maybe he would understand, and you could talk about all of this with him after I tell him. Regardless of what you did, brah, you are still our fucking father, and that's *that*."

I told him the police have a grandfathered rule that you could rejoin society if you have a late stage of cancer, if you were an exemplary prisoner. I was known as inmate 6765-098 and I hated every minute of being away from my sons. I told them, "I thought about you every day in there; you have no idea how bad I wanted to call and have your mama come and bring you up there. In the end, what good would that have done? It was selfish as fuck and I know that I can't go back and change the past. As much as I want to, I just can't change that past, son, and I'm hoping you can forgive me for all the times I wasn't there. I have done some fucked up things I'm not proud of and, hell, I'll probably still end up doing some things that are not good, but I will try. I just want you to do me a favor and not tell Lil Mike; I would like to be the one that tell him if that's okay." He said nothing; he just nodded and kept drinking his beer. Now the feds wanted me to tell on both of my sons, and I just couldn't do it. I would create an allusion I would set them both up, but how could I leave this fucking earth knowing I was the cause of both of my sons incarcerated like some fucking dogs?

He said, "Let me ask you one more question: What about all these brothers and sisters I am supposed to have?" I looked at him and said, "You have another older brother and a younger sister, and the other kids are not mine. I can introduce you one day if you would like. They were in the same boat as you guys because I didn't want any of my kids to see me like that in that jail."

He shook his head and said he understood. He gave me a pound and told me to keep my head up and my secret was safe with him. I told him I would get with him the next day to check on him and his brother. We both agreed. As soon as they left, my phone went off, and I already knew who it was because my handler was this black dude. After all, they didn't want to make it suspicious with a white man following me around. He asked me what I said to my son and I told him I am making progress. I had a recorder under my shirt, and I hated the shit: I mean every minute of it. Even though I was free, hell, I wasn't near free. I told him I would work on my son and he reminded me I didn't have the time he thinks I had, and I needed to hurry the fuck up. I would do the best I could to make this right and make sure my sons are good from there on out.

Chapter 34

Lil Mike

As I sat in the cell and contemplated what my brother told me and how the fuck was a piece of tin going to land me in jail, I remember I burned that fucking car to a crisp and thought I covered my tracks well. As I sat back and played the night over that I killed Alicia, I thought about every detail. From me picking her up in the front of her house, the restaurant and her giving me head to where I blew her fucking brains out the back of her skull. I felt some remorse, but she was the enemy 's cousin and I just couldn't have that knowing she was probably setting me up the entire time. I had to, that's what was replaying in the back of my head. I needed to clear my mind, so I walked out to the rec room and these niggas were staring at me like I was fresh meat. Yeah, this was only my second time in jail, but I wasn't no fucking punk, so I hope nobody thought they were about to try shit. I was up that bitch alone true enough, but, fuck it, I could hold my own with the best of them. I noticed a few niggas I robbed in here but they did not understand who I was because we were always careful, well mostly, but we robbed people we didn't think deserved to have what they had. It wasn't a great profession, but, hell, you do what you must do. I didn't regret shit but meeting Alicia and my brother robbing Head without me knowing about it. I walked down the hall and a few niggas were still staring at me, so I said fuck it and asked if we had a fucking problem. This nigga named Freddie asked me if I knew a nigga name Antonio and said that I am the spitting image of him. I said, "No, should I know the nigga?"

"It must be your fucking daddy then, nigga."

I said, "I don't know nobody named fucking Antonio. It didn't ring a bell, nor do I fuck with that many niggas to not know who or remember a nigga named Antonio." A few days went by and I was still wondering if I knew a nigga named Antonio. I called my brother about the lawyer and he told me he said he's working on the case as much as he can. I didn't have a public defender so I told him to tell that nigga to hurry up and get me the fuck up out of there, and, before I hung up, I asked my brother if he and Brian knew a nigga named Antonio and to search around. I hung up with Josh and then Freddie walked by and I told him to come to my cell for a hot second. I asked, "Why did you ask me about that nigga the other day?" He proceeded to tell me that he ratted out his brother and his brother wanted revenge on the nigga who did it. I said I did not know a rat because I don't associate with fucking rats.

He said, "No disrespect, bro, but you got his whole face." I said to myself *they can't be talking about Big Mike because his name is Michael Beasly, Sr. because I'm junior, so it just can't be him.* Also, when the fuck did he even find the time to do a stint in jail when that nigga couldn't come see us. He was probably with his other kids and treating them fucking kids good. I bet he played football with them and went to every football game. Oh well, that wasn't the case for me because I had to take care of my little brother and mama. So, about three days later, Freddie came in my cell and asked if I was busy, and I told that nigga to come in and he showed me a picture of Big Mike in that picture dapping up some big strong nigga standing beside him.

I said, "Naw, we just look alike, that's all." I needed to do some more digging and research because that was him in that picture as clear as day. I asked Freddie what happened again, and he ran it down to me that Antonio snitched on his brother and got him more time. I almost said that my fucking daddy ain't no rat, but I didn't know if Freddie was just scheming on like it didn't feel right about the situation. On top of that, my fucking brother wasn't answering the phone for no one and no one had seen him. It fucked with me when I couldn't get a hold of him. So, I got a little tighter with Freddie and I'd been locked up for two months and had yet to receive a court date. *This is really some bullshit,* I said to nobody. Freddie busted in my cell and told me he had proof that Antonio was my father.

"Why the fuck would you lie, nigga, and I been keeping it real with you, bro. These niggas don't care about you! This is a jail." I told him he was right about everything. He sat on my bed and told me, "This is you and your pops, right? He is a snitch, man, and now they couldn't get any more information." I told him to not say a fucking word about this. I asked him if I could get a copy of that paper-work with Antonio's name and face on it. As I laid on my bunk, I punched the air and realized that I needed to get out of there as soon as possible. My Dad was a fucking snitch.

Thanks to everybody and I hope you enjoyed this first book. Part Two is coming and I hope you know there will be more twists and turns. I would like to thank everybody who purchased the book. I've been working on this book for seven years and got it done.

www.ingramcontent.com/pod-product-compliance
Lightning Source LLC
Chambersburg PA
CBHW051145020726
47501CB00005B/1695